D0295883

Praise for
THE WIZARD IN MY SHED

'The book made me laugh so much I was
silent laughing' TOPPSTA REVIEWER, AGED 9

'I absolutely loved this book'
TOPPSTA REVIEWER, AGED 8

'This book is amazing … [it] has earned a special
place …' TOPPSTA REVIEWER, AGED 10

'Really funny' SUMMER, AGED 12

'Very funny and original'
JOHNNY, AGED 12, BOOKS UP NORTH

'A time-travelling comedy of errors
full of mischief' GUARDIAN

'A hoot of a debut' OBSERVER

'[Delivers] plenty of laughs' SUNDAY EXPRESS

'Big-hearted, inventive and very,
very funny' BOOKTRUST

'Made me laugh out loud on more than
one occasion' READINGZONE

THE WARRIOR IN MY WARDROBE

MORE MISADVENTURES of MERDYN the WILD!

ILLUSTRATED BY CLAIRE POWELL

SIMON FARNABY

h HODDER

First published in Great Britain in 2021 by Hodder & Stoughton

1 3 5 7 9 10 8 6 4 2

Text copyright © Simon Farnaby, 2021
Illustrations copyright © Claire Powell, 2021

The moral right of the author has been asserted.

All characters and events in this publication, other than those clearly
in the public domain, are fictitious and any resemblance to
real persons, living or dead, is purely coincidental.

All rights reserved.
No part of this publication may be reproduced, stored in a retrieval system,
or transmitted, in any form or by any means, without the prior permission in
writing of the publisher, nor be otherwise circulated in any form of binding or
cover other than that in which it is published and without a similar condition
including this condition being imposed on the subsequent purchaser.

A CIP catalogue record for this book
is available from the British Library.

HB ISBN 978 1 444 95880 5
Trade PB ISBN 978 1 444 95464 7

Typeset in Archetype
Printed and bound in Great Britain by Clays Ltd, Elcograf S.p.A

The paper and board used in this book
are made from wood from responsible sources.

MIX
Paper from
responsible sources
FSC
www.fsc.org   FSC® C104740

LONDON BOROUGH OF RICHMOND UPON THAMES DISCARDED	
90710 000 491 172	
Askews & Holts	03-Nov-2021
JF	
RTES	

For Edie

CHAPTER ONE

SIBLINGS FALL OUT AND ROSE HAS SELF-DOUBT

Rose Falvey was in the garden shed at 23 Daffodil Close, Bashingford, tending to an injured parrot. It had been a year since Merdyn the Wild had gone back to the Dark Ages and since then her makeshift veterinary clinic had cured countless dogs, cats, hamsters and tortoises of various minor ailments and injuries using Rose's newfound magic powers. She used a pinecone spell so that the animals could talk to her and tell her what was wrong.

Her best friend and chief scientist Tamsin helped her out and nothing gave them greater pleasure than seeing a stricken pet walk out on their feet/paws. All they asked of the animals' owners was a voluntary donation to pay for the herbs they needed for spells (the type of magic Rose was capable of required a chanted spell PLUS a liberal scattering of herbs). School was going well, the vet clinic was going well, she had a cool, brainy best friend – everything in Rose's life was tickety-boo. There was only one problem. A problem that reared its ugly head (or pretty head, I should say) the very Saturday morning that you, our reader, joins this story. The problem was . . .

KRIS.

Rose was just mending the parrot's leg with a bone-fixing spell (it had been chased around the front room by the family cat and caught its foot in the fireguard) when she heard an almighty explosion outside in the garden.

She burst out of the shed door to find her older brother Kris standing in the middle of the lawn performing some sort of magic show to twenty or so of his annoying schoolfriends.

"And now for Invisiboy's signature spell!" he crowed.

"PASSIFLORA INVISIBLATA!"

Kris then threw dried passion-flower petals over himself and promptly disappeared, much the audience's delight.

You see, Kris could also do magic. Those of you who

read the last book in this series (and if you haven't, what is WRONG with you?) will know that Rose found out she was related to Merdyn the Wild and so was a W-blood (wizard, witch or warlock). And Kris soon realised that if Rose could do magic, then so could he. How Kris used his powers, however, couldn't have been more different to how Rose used hers.

While Rose used her magic to help injured hedgehogs, Kris used his to help him hog the limelight! He loved to show off. He would produce lightning from his fingers and use the levitation spell to show off in front of girls down the shopping centre. He would make himself invisible to get into football matches and music concerts for free. He'd even started wearing a superhero outfit and had come up with a list of names.

1. LIGHTNING BOY!
2. MAGIC MAN!
3. AMAZITEEN!
4. THE BIG WOW!
5. FANTASTIKID!
6. THE INCREDIBLE KRIS!
7. PSYCHO-KID!
   (I don't think he'd thought this one through, do you?)
8. THE BIG HALLOOBY!
   (Your guess is as good as mine . . .)
9. FALVEY THE FABULOUS!
10. SUPERBOY!

As Rose watched Kris showing off in the garden that morning, she thought of a more appropriate name for him.

"Oi, Idiotboy!" she called out.

Kris rematerialised in front of the crowd. "It's Invisiboy!" he huffed angrily.

"I don't care who you are, we had a deal, remember? You don't put on stupid magic shows while my vet clinic is open."

"Boo!" A couple of boys shouted at Rose as if it were a pantomime.

"And you lot can shut up and get out of my garden," Rose rasped back at them, not exactly helping to dispel their belief that she was the villain.

"But your dumb vet clinic is ALWAYS open, like ALL weekend!" Kris complained. "So when am I supposed to do my magic shows?"

"I dunno!" Rose said, exasperated. "At school? On the street? Or how about never at all? You shouldn't use magic to entertain; you should use it to help people. With great power comes great responsibility." Rose regretting saying this sentence almost as soon as it had left her mouth. She liked the phrase and she meant it, but it was from the movie *Spider-Man* and she was worried someone might notice.

"That's from *Spider-Man*," said a small kid

with glasses.

"I don't care if it's from the land of the Wizard of Oz!" Rose countered. "Take your magic show elsewhere! I have a parrot's life to save." And with that she stomped angrily into her shed. Kris told his friends to go home and stormed off to his room.

I'm afraid that the event I just described for you had become commonplace in the Falvey household since Merdyn had left. There is no easy way of putting it, dear reader.

THE SIBLINGS WERE AT WAR!

As far as Rose was concerned it was all Kris's fault. He had let his powers go to his head and become a complete hufty tufty*.

For Kris it was Rose who was causing all the problems. Since she'd saved the world from Jerabo the Great and his sneaky son Julian Smith in the battle of Stonehenge, Rose had become no fun at all. All she wanted to do was mend animals and talk about responsibility. Boooooring!

Kris was so angry with his sister for spoiling his fun that he had vowed to prove himself better than Rose at

----

*An old word for "show off". I told you, you should have read the last book!

magic. And so he came up with new, exciting spells that she couldn't perform. The invisibility spell was one of them, and he had recently perfected a memory-wipe spell.

Rose was furious as she had been trying to perfect that spell for ages but just couldn't get it right. Stupid Kris had mastered it in weeks! Even more annoying was that he wouldn't share it with her. It would have been soooo useful in her vet clinic. She could get cats to forget being traumatised by dogs, and dogs to forget being traumatised by cats. But would Kris share it? No. Kris didn't see why he should share it when she wouldn't give him the pinecone spell that Rose used to allow her pet guinea pig, Bubbles, to speak. He wanted to use it on a wasp, which Rose thought was ridiculous (and so did Bubbles).

What annoyed Rose most – although she hated to admit it – was that deep down she knew she just wasn't as good at magic as Kris. I mean, yes, she'd saved the world once, but she had had Merdyn to help her then, the greatest wizard of all time. On her own she was just a mediocre W-blood at best, and she hated Kris for spelling it out (literally) so clearly for her.

Rose's beloved father, who had died a few years ago, had always told Rose that she would do something special with her life, would BE something special. When she found out she could do magic, she'd thought that was it! THIS was what her father had meant! But now Kris could do magic too. Not only that, he could do magic BETTER than her. Well, what made her so special now? Nothing. These were the thoughts that went through her head every night and which would keep her awake until she cried herself to sleep.

"Would you mind keeping the noise down please?" a voice would often pipe up from the cage in the corner of her bedroom. There sat a yellow guinea pig, munching on muesli.

The voice
was from Bubbles,
A beloved pet
who didn't care for troubles.

CHAPTER TWO

WRITER'S BLOCK
AND
LIGHTNING SHOCKS!

Caught in the middle of her warring children was their poor mum Suzy. It was the last thing she needed. She was having problems of her own! She had started singing again recently. She was doing gigs to hundreds of people, singing songs from her old band The Mondays, but the fans wouldn't keep coming back for the same six songs. She needed some new tracks but was struggling with writer's block.

One quiet Sunday morning she was on the verge of completing a wonderful new song. It was called "Mother's on the Verge of a Nervous Breakdown" and was about a tired mum who had writer's block and was sick of her kids fighting (I don't know where she got that idea from, do you?). She had just begun to write the lyrics, the words spilling from her pen on to the paper, when she heard an argument erupt down the corridor.

"Keep out of my room!" screamed Kris.

"I don't want to BE in your room!" Rose yelled back. "I just want the spell!"

Suzy put her earplugs in, which had been bought especially for these occasions. *Ah, that's better*, she thought and carried on writing.

Meanwhile, the argument was escalating. That morning Rose had begged Kris for the millionth time to let her have the memory-wipe spell. She'd had someone bring in a pet rabbit who'd had a bag of carrots fall on its head and it was now traumatised by the sight of carrots. But they were the only things that it liked eating, so now it was starving to death.

Kris tried to bargain with her. "I'll lend it to you if I can do magic shows ALL DAY Saturday."

"Saturday's our busiest day!" Rose protested.

"Then no memory-wipe spell," Kris sang in an annoying whiny voice that he knew really wound Rose up.

"Look, *stupid hair boy*," Rose hit back, using the one thing SHE knew would wind him up: any criticism whatsoever of his hair. (Kris was a little vain; he had so much hairspray in it he needed to keep at least ten metres away from candles or it would burst into flames.) "I'm going to create my own memory-wipe spell soon. And guess what? It'll be WAY better than yours . . ."

"That's fine then!" Kris cut in. "You don't need mine!"

Rose lost her temper. "But I need it now! A rabbit is starving to death!"

"You know what the real problem is here, Rose," Kris retorted, still smarting from the hair comment. "You just can't stand that I'm better at magic than you!"

"WHAT?!!" Rose yelled back in fake disgust, "You wouldn't even know you could DO magic if it wasn't for me."

Kris had spotted a weakness. "That's not the point!

The point is I'm better at it than you and you hate it."

"I am WAY better than you!" his sister yelled.

"Then do your own spells and stop embarrassing yourself by begging for mine!" Kris shouted back.

"I'll tell you what I really hate if you must know." Rose had never been angrier in her life. "YOU, Kris! I hate YOU! I wish I'd never had a brother!"

"Ha!" Kris laughed in her face. "You think I want *you* as a sister!? A boring goody two shoes!!"

At that moment something inside Rose snapped. Without thinking she reached for some dill leaves from a pouch in the herb belt round her waist and threw a lightning spell.

"HOLCUS CRACKAJACKA!"

she screamed as she threw the dill leaves, and white electric streams crackled from her fingers and whizzed past Kris's head, singeing the left side of his hair.

KABOOM!

The ferocity of the explosion blew Kris's door off its hinges and incinerated the contents of his room: bed, duvet, trendy retro record player, hair products and hairdryers (one for every different hairstyle) – the lot – then smashed a two-metre circular hole in the far wall.

"Oh . . . MY . . . GOD!!" exclaimed Kris and immediately ran downstairs and into the garden. Rose knew what he was going to do and followed him, shouting, "Nononononononononono!"

Rose got to the garden just as Kris was throwing HIS dill leaves over Rose's beloved shed.

"HOLCUS CRACKAJACKA!"

he yelled and – BOOM! – of course his lightning spell was even more powerful than Rose's and the wooden shed was blasted from its concrete base UP INTO THE AIR!

As it flew vertically into the sky and came crashing down in a heap of crumpled wood and veterinary instruments, Rose found herself jealous that even Kris's blooming lightning spells were better than hers!

"RIGHT!! THAT'S IT!!!" came a voice from behind the children. The voice was Mum's. The noise from the two explosions had finally penetrated the earplugs and she was now standing in the garden in front of the twin destroyers of her home. "I'm banning magic from this house! For six months! And if I hear one word of complaint, it'll be **FOR EVER!**"

Kris started to complain. "But—"

"Shut up, Kris!" snapped Rose.

"*Me* shut up?" Kris retorted. "This is all your fault."

"ENOUGH!!" Suzy bellowed. The bickering siblings fell silent. "No magic for six months. And you can *both* share the blame! It's just about the only thing you *can* share!"

Upstairs in Rose's room, Bubbles had been listening to the whole farrago with faint amusement. Humans were so complicated, he thought. They want for so much. He was happy with a bowl of organic pet-shop grains and a snooze.

Magic should have brought joy
to their life.
Instead it had brought
trouble and strife.

CHAPTER THREE

SURPRISE! THESE PAGES RETURN TO THE DARK AGES ...

The year 521 to be precise. Ten years after Merdyn had returned from the future. But we're not going to see your favourite warlock-turned-wizard just yet. We're not in Bashingford now! Far from it. We're in what is now Romania. *Transylvania* to be precise (again) . . .

Transylvania in the Dark Ages was a land in turmoil. The Romans had conquered the place and then been thrown out by the Vandals*, who in turn had been thrown out by the Goths**.

There was such upheaval that by the year 521 nobody really knew who was in charge, so it ended up being home

----

*The Vandals were from Germania (modern-day Germany) and they quite enjoyed sticking it to the Romans, often smashing up their beautiful buildings and artwork just for the heck of it (hence the term "vandalism").

**"Goth" derives from two tribes, the Visigoths and the Ostrogoths, who invaded the Roman Empire in the second and third centuries. Today the word is often associated with music and fashion. A "goth" is characterised as someone drawn to mystery, horror and gloom. The Romans would certainly agree with that!

to various waifs and strays who had been chased out of other countries and didn't really know where to go. One such person was Vanheldon – king of the Vandals.

Vanheldon was an imposing battle-hardened warrior with thick matted hair and a long wiry beard that made it look like a giant hedge on legs was running towards you. He had small dark eyes set into his grey craggy face like two caves in a mountain slope. His nose had been broken so many times it looked more like a potato. He wore llama-skin boots on his feet, deer-skin trousers on his legs, a bear-skin tunic covered his barrel-like chest, and he had a necklace adorned with tiger teeth and dried dead rats. To top it off he wore a leather helmet on his head with bull horns sticking out of it. It was fair to say he was NOT a vegetarian!

Vanheldon had once commanded hundreds of soldiers. But one day he led an invasion of Albion (England) and had his entire army destroyed by one man. That man's name was . . . Merdyn the Wild.

The Vandal king went back to mainland Europe with only his daughter Vanhessa, a couple of guards and a trunk full of his dead soldiers' belongings. He roamed from place to place before eventually settling in what became Transylvania. The weather there suited him, because it was dark, broody and unpredictable. There he cleared an area of woodland on the top of a hill above a small village and built a sinister-looking fortress*. It was square in shape with a courtyard in the centre and a watchtower in the middle of one side adorned with giant wooden bull horns. The whole building was surrounded by a fence of sharpened wooden stakes on top of which he placed various dead animals' heads. This was a decoration that would be copied nearly a thousand years later by Transylvania's other famous son, Vlad the Impaler**.

If the animal heads on sticks didn't put off unwanted visitors, then its name would. Vanheldon called his home Fort Doom. And day after day, week after week, month after month, Vanheldon would pace up and down the courtyard of Fort Doom plotting revenge on

---

*He would have built a castle but stone castles wouldn't be invented until the twelfth century, so he built a wooden fortress instead.

**Vlad the Impaler became ruler of Romania in 1436. His father's name was Dracul, which meant that Vlad was also known as Dracula (son of Dracul) – so no guessing which famous horror character was named after him! (Count Dracula, the vampire – are you keeping up? What are you doing down here? Get back to the action!)

Merdyn the Wild.

Eventually, after years of brooding, mulling and thinking, Vanheldon finally unveiled his cunning revenge plan to his daughter at dinner one night.

"I have decided, I am going to killeth him," he grunted as he scoffed a bowl of pottage***.

Vanhessa coughed up some pottage. She'd been expecting a better plan than this.

"Hmm. Good idea, Father," she said, her expression telling a different story. "Have thou given any thought as to how thou might killeth him?"

"Of course I HAVE!" Vanheldon bellowed angrily and thumped his fist upon the table. "With a BIG KNIFE! Ha ha ha ha!" He took his HUGE hunting knife from its sheath and threw it at the far wall where it stuck out like a coat peg.

"Father, if I may be so bold—" began Vanhessa, but her father interrupted.

"Bald? Thou art not bald, Vanhessa. Thou have a fine

***Pottage is another word for stew. This was basically all anyone ate in the Dark Ages. Beans, vegetables and (if you were rich) meat would be boiled together in a pot as this was the best use of firewood. So next time you complain about having some nice steamed broccoli lathered in butter, just remember it sure beats pottage!

head of hair, the most bountiful in all the lands!"

It was true. Vanhessa did have a lovely thick head of hair. In fact, everything about Vanhessa was impressive. She had legs like two tree trunks and her arms bulged with muscles like a sea snake that's swallowed a camel. Her face was the spitting image of her father's except she had green eyes instead of mud-brown and a smaller less broken nose. Her eyebrows were less like hedgerows too, more like long thin caterpillars, and they were usually highly arched, especially when she was listening to one of her father's plans.

"No, Father, I said if I may be so *bold*, ahem, I think it would be a *mistake* to try to killeth Merdyn the Wild on our own. Remember, we had nearly a thousand soldiers when we invaded Albion – now we have two."

"Bah!!" Vanheldon thumped the table again. If you were in the room, dear reader, you would have noticed a small indentation in the table under Vanheldon's fist, suggesting that he thumps his table A LOT. "What do you suggesteth then, daughter?!"

"Well, Merdyn is W-Blood. So, I suggest we try to

find someone who is W-blood to help us defeateth him."

The cogs in the machine of poor Vanheldon's battle-bruised brain began to whirr and crank to life as they got to grips with his daughter's suggestion.

"Huh. I am glad thou have thy mother's brains, Vanhessa," he grunted, his face turning sad as he recalled his much-loved wife. "If only she hadn't been eaten by that bear, thou and she would have madeth a goodly team."

And so Vanheldon let it be known that he was searching for a W-blood that would help him get his revenge on Merdyn the Wild. He set up a stage in the fort's courtyard to hold auditions, and as a reward he offered up his casket full of gold and silver trinkets, which had belonged to his dead soldiers – the spoils of war*.

This turned out to be a mistake, however. He may as well have asked for every crackpot and oddball in the area to come to his fort and perform cheap magic tricks. After six weeks of watching people pretend to pull rabbits out of caps and disappear behind curtains, there wasn't a genuine magician among them. He angrily called off the search,

----

*In the Dark Ages whenever an army attacked a place it would steal money, treasures or valuables of any kind and keep them. That way they could pay for more weapons and armour for even more wars. This is called looting, and what they take is known as the spoils of war.

exclaiming, "I will never have revenge on that cursed Merdyn!!"

As he stomped back to his room, he nearly fell over an old beggar woman, bent double and hobbling with a walking stick.

"Excuseth me, sire . . ." she said weakly.

But Vanheldon was in no mood for beggars. "Out of my way, peasant! I have no time for charity . . ."

"But, sire . . ."

"I said be gone!!" In his wrath he pulled a club out of his belt, a club that he had nicknamed his "beggar beater" (for reasons that ought to be self-evident) and which he was about to bring down upon the poor old lady when . . . WHOOSH!

With one gesture of the old lady's finger the club flew out of Vanheldon's hand, past Vanhessa's head and tonked against the wall at the far end of the courtyard. Vanheldon's mouth fell open like the drawbridge of a castle that hadn't been invented yet.

"Thou art . . . W-W-W-blood?" stuttered the fearsome Vandal.

"Aye," spoke the witch, and she pulled the scraggly hair from her face. Beneath all the mud and dirt she had piercing blue eyes under thin black eyebrows that pointed sharply downwards towards a long slender nose that looked like it had been made from porcelain, then covered with soot.

"Druilla be my name. And I will help thee getteth revenge on Merdyn the Wild."

"If thou doest this, there will be a chest of treasures waiting for thee."

"I needeth not trinkets and baubles," said Druilla confidently. "Killing Merdyn the Wild shall be a reward in itself."

"What quarrel do thou have with Merdyn the Wild?"

asked the inquisitive Vanhessa, sensing there was more to this story.

The old witch's eyes flashed brightly, like two bright blue sapphires in a coal mine. "My reasons are mine own," she said mysteriously.

"Who careth for reasons!" bellowed Vanheldon. "Prepareth the horses! We leaveth for Albion this very night!"

But Druilla didn't move. "Oh, please, I am an old woman," she said. "All that travelling. No, no, no. We shall let Merdyn cometh to us."

Vanheldon paused a moment to take this in, then burst out laughing. "Ha ha. Ya ya ya! Let Merdyn cometh to us?! Art thou a jester, woman? Where art thy funny hat and bells?! Merdyn would sooner jumpeth into a volcano. Ha ha. Why on this great flat earth would Merdyn cometh to us?"

"Because we shall have someone he loves."

Now even the much smarter Vanhessa was confused.

"What do thou meaneth? His wife Evanhart?" she enquired of the witch. "His children? We could not get near them. Merdyn's magic is too powerful."

Now it was Druilla's turn to laugh. It was a throaty witch's cackle, as you would expect.

"Oh, dear me. Have ye not heard the stories of Merdyn's adventures through the Rivers of Time?"

Vanhessa and Vanheldon looked at each other and shrugged.

"Hmm. I might have guessed thou did not tell your daughter bedtime stories, Vanheldon," crowed Druilla a little condescendingly, Vanhessa thought. "If thou had thine ears open to the tittle-tattle* thou would have known that there is another Merdyn loves. She goeth by the name of . . . Rose. She liveth some two thousand years into the future, in a place called Bashingford."

"And how are we supposed to travelleth to the future?" asked Vanheldon, his heavy eyebrows knitting together like a huge black woolly scarf.

"Not 'we'," remarked Druilla. "A journey into the future is far too perilous for me."

---

*Tittle-tattle is gossip and was often how stories were spread. It was known as the oral tradition. Even though the earliest books were written in roughly 2000 BC they weren't widely circulated. The first printing press was built in 1454 by a German man called Johannes Gutenburg. So thanks, Johannes!!

Vanheldon thought for a minute before rephrasing his question.

"All right then, how is *she* –" he pointed to his daughter – "going to travelleth to the future?"

Vanhessa looked stunned. How the heck had she been volunteered for this?!

"Do not worry," Druilla reassured them. "I have a spell that can transport her."

My, how Vanhessa
looked in confusion.
Through the Rivers of Time
she must make an intrusion.

CHAPTER FOUR

IMAGINARY DIARIES
AND
CRIMINAL ENQUIRIES

Unlike the feuding Rose and Kris, Bubbles had been very happy since Merdyn had gone back to the Dark Ages. For a start he had a pinecone attached to a little collar round his neck so that Rose and whoever else was interested could hear his thoughts on a permanent basis. Not many pets are afforded this luxury and, my, what a difference to an animal's life it makes! Rose had given Bubbles a Dictaphone to record his thoughts in. Every day he would talk into it. It was a sort of audio diary. Bubbles dreamed that one day after he was long dead someone would find it and write a book about all his genius thoughts. And the book would be called *The Secret Diary of Bubbles the Guinea Pig Aged Two(ish)*.

On the day Rose and Kris were banned from using magic, a sunny Sunday in the school summer holidays,

Bubbles pressed record on the Dictaphone and listed all the good things about being able to talk . . .

Right. Shhh. Quiet. OK. Here goes . . . Ahem.

1. Food. Being able to talk means I can ask Rose for any kind of food I want. At the moment I'm into organic muesli from the posh pet shop in town. It's ace.

2. Poos. The organic muesli keeps my poos nice and regular, which is what guinea pigs are good at. One poo every seven minutes is ideal for me. Soft fresh fruit makes me poo far too regularly – say, once every four minutes, which is just too often and makes life all about poo. It's all poo, poo, poo, poo, poo, and no one needs that, not even a guinea pig. Now, non-organic muesli makes me poo every ten minutes, which is far *too long* to wait and makes me feel anxious. So being able to ask for my favourite muesli is very important. This one is really to do with food

again, but I didn't just want to talk about food all the time.

3. Food. Being able to talk also lets me tell other animals to stay away from my food. While I'm in the garden or at the shops with my owner Rose, birds, cats and even dogs will often try to eat my food. I tell them to "get lost" and they tend to freak out because they've never heard a guinea pig talk before. So that's another good thing. Right.

4. Dogs. Did I mention I hate dogs? And when I say I hate them, I mean I HAAAAAATE them. I HAAAAATE THEM. I, I, I HAAAAAAATE them so much. I mean, HAAAAA— You get the picture. I hate *everything* about them. Their slobbery mouths and unreasonably wet noses. Why are their noses so wet? What's all that about? D'you know what I mean?! *My* nose isn't wet! And what's worse is that they poke their

noses into everyone else's business. And they think they're sooooo great because they can run fast and bark and stuff. I haaaate them! I think I said that. I like being able to talk so I can tell dogs to get lost and freak them out. I did mention this in number 3 but I just wanted to say it again because I cannot tell you how much I HAAAATE dogs.

5. Food. Being able to ask for food is good.

6. Poos. I might have mentioned poos. But being able to talk is good for my poos because being able to talk means I can control my food. So, poos. And what else? Oh yes.

7. Did I mention that I hate dogs? Well, I do, I HAAAAAATE them. The end.

Bubbles had only just finished his list when Rose rushed in, looking flustered.

"I just finished a great diary entry," he told her. But she wasn't listening. She was looking intently at a piece of paper in her hand and eagerly muttering the words written on it.

Bubbles knew what a spell sounded like by now: a load of weird nonsense words. He also knew what Rose's handwriting looked like and this wasn't it. In fact, if he'd had to guess he'd say it was *Kris's* handwriting on that piece of paper, and now Rose was furtively hiding it at the bottom of a drawer.

"Erm, excuse me!!?" the rodent shouted in his loudest voice.

Rose jumped a guilty jump. "Oh, Bubbles. You scared me!"

Bubbles glared at her suspiciously. "Oh yes? And why's that?"

Rose stuttered guiltily. "Erm, er, because I didn't know you were there."

"But I'm always here," said Bubbles, now looking Rose in the eye. "That piece of paper you've just hidden doesn't belong to you, does it?"

Rose looked back at him, then her eyes darted to the floor, a sign that she was ashamed.

"It belongs to *Kris*, doesn't it?" Bubbles said calmly in a way that told Rose she didn't need to answer. "It's one of his spells, isn't it? And you've stolen it, haven't you?" Rose nodded slowly. "Come on. What spell is it?"

"It's . . . the memory-wipe spell," she admitted.

"Rose Falvey," uttered Bubbles, very much in the tone of a disappointed parent or grandparent or teacher, "what has happened to you?"

Rose protested. "Look! Kris wouldn't even know he had magic powers if it wasn't for me. *I* found Merdyn. *I* helped him get home. Kris is just . . . riding on my coat-tails! Just think how much a memory-wipe spell could help my animals. It could help *you* forget you hate dogs!"

Bubbles fumed. "I don't want to forget I hate dogs! I want to remember for ever and ever. It's good I hate dogs. It stops me being eaten by them. I LIKE hating dogs."

Rose sighed. "You know what I mean. I could use it to help, you know, *normal* animals."

"And so you thought you'd steal it."

"It's for the greater good."

"For the 'greater good'?" said Bubbles. "Is that another quote from Spidersman?"

"It's *Spider-Man*." Rose corrected.

"Whatever!" Bubbles was in no mood for spelling corrections. "You're on thin ice, Rose Falvey. Magic has already been banned from this house, and that affects me. Without magic I can't talk! So you might want to think about other people's feelings before you get magic banned from this house for ever and I'll have to go and live with . . ." Bubbles couldn't think of another W-blood apart from Rose and Kris. Then he remembered. "Uncle Martin!"

Uncle Martin was Rose's uncle, who was also a descendant of Merdyn the Wild and therefore capable of magic. Though he chose not to, instead living a quiet life in the Highlands of Scotland with "the magic of the landscape", as he called it.

"Point is, you've changed, Rose," Bubbles summed up. "You're not having a midlife crisis, are you?" He was just repeating a phrase he'd heard on television, but it was worth a shot.

"Of course I'm not having a midlife crisis!" Rose replied. "I'm twelve. It's just . . . I can't believe he's better than me at magic."

Finally, thought Bubbles, the truth was out. Then he did something that he didn't really like to do; he gave Rose some friendly advice.

"He's not better than you, Rose. He's just different. And you wouldn't want him stealing one of *your* spells, would you?"

Rose shook her head. "No."

"Then do the right thing and go and put it back."

Rose sighed the sigh of a girl who knows when her pet guinea pig is talking sense. She took the piece of paper from the drawer, then stood up and turned to face Bubbles. "You're right," she said calmly.

"I'm glad you've seen sense," replied Bubbles, pleased with himself.

"But I'm afraid I just can't give it back . . ."

Bubbles looked at Rose with a "what the wha—?" expression on his furry face, but before he could speak Rose blurted out the words on the piece of paper.

"PRIMULA VERIS THINKSWIPEYMEMORALIS!"

Then she flung some herbs over Bubbles's cage and PIFF!

All was silent.

Bubbles's vacant eyes stared for a moment then blinked. Then he twitched his nose. Waggled his whiskers. "Huh. Erm. What were we talking about?" he asked Rose.

"Oh, nothing." Rose slid the spell in the bottom drawer again, this time taking care to NOT let Bubbles see what she was doing. "You were just telling me how you hate dogs."

"Oh, I do," said Bubbles, satisfied that the conversation was back on track. "I do sooo much. I HAAAATE dogs. I HAAAAATE them." And with that he went back to munching on his organic muesli and squeezed out a poo.

*Rose had dodged
a Bubbles guilt bullet,
But would Kris soon find out
whodunnit?*

CHAPTER FIVE

SHE TRAVELS THROUGH THE RIVERS – TO GIVE YOU THE SHIVERS!

It was a warm summer day when Vanhessa Vanheldon finally arrived in Daffodil Close, Bashingford. It had been two weeks since the young warrior had been "volunteered" by her father to travel into the Rivers of Time.

When Vanhessa had arrived in modern-day Transylvania, Fort Doom was gone and where it used to be there were people dressed in strange short trousers and using tools to dig up the ground (you and I would know it as an archaeology dig).

A young bespectacled archaeologist marched angrily up to the warrior daughter of a sixth-century Vandal king.

"Hey. You're not supposed to be here yet!" she yelled. "And move away from that area; we found a suit of armour there."

Vanhessa looked down at her feet to see the rusty

breastplate of a suit of armour.

"No skeleton, though, weirdly," added the archaeologist before turning to Vanhessa again. "Go on, scram – we don't need the re-enactors until Friday."

Vanhessa didn't know what "scram" meant but she knew when someone was being rude, so she picked the archaeologist up with one hand and threw her, like a rag doll, fully ten metres into a pile of freshly dug soil.

"Which way is Albion?" she then asked the rest of the rather fearful archaeology team. One of them scrambled for their smartphone, found out that Albion was now called England and looked on a map before pointing decisively north-west.

"Thankings," Vanhessa said politely, before stomping off.

Vanhessa was used to walking or "marching" as warriors called it. She had once marched all over Europe, conquering and killing and generally causing mayhem. But her job this time was just to grab a little girl, put her in a sack and carry her back to the spot where she had arrived in exactly one month. Easy.

Two weeks later, Vanhessa was striding down Daffodil Close on the bright summer Sunday I mentioned in a previous chapter.

"Rose Falvey?" Vanhessa asked a friendly neighbour walking down the street. The neighbour looked Vanhessa up and down – taking in the furs, pelts, horned helmet and . . . the smell! – before pointing to Rose's house.

"Although her vet clinic is closed temporarily if that's what you're after. Mind you, even she would have a job bringing those back to life," said the cheery neighbour, referencing the decorative necklace of dried rats that Vanhessa had hanging round her neck.

Vanhessa hadn't a clue what he was talking about, but had worked out it was best to just grunt "thankyou" at these modern people and march on.

Inside the Falvey family house everyone was out except Kris. Suzy had taken Rose swimming and Kris was in his partially rebuilt bedroom making a list of his spells and listening to some very loud rap music on his headphones. If the music hadn't been so loud, he might have heard the front door being kicked off its hinges by a Vandal warrior.

Vanhessa searched downstairs for Rose. Not really knowing how people lived in this strange modern world, she pulled cupboard doors off hinges, looked in the oven and even toppled the fridge over and cleft it in two with her broadsword. There was no little girl in there but there was a tasty-looking rib-eye steak that she devoured in one hungry bite.

SCRUMP!

Next Vanhessa found the stairs and climbed up them. She looked in Suzy's room before checking the bathroom where she took a drink from the water bowl (toilet to you and me), then her eyes rested on something familiar – a sign on a door in the corridor saying

ROSE'S ROOM – KEEP OUT!!

She peered at it and then at the shapes Druilla had drawn in mud on her arm. Vanhessa couldn't read*, but she could make out a two-handled-axe, a circle, a snake and a pitch fork.

R . . . O . . . S . . . E.

----

*In the Dark Ages the only people who could read were the very rich or members of the church. Literacy only really became common in the eighteenth and nineteenth century, and even now around 14% of the world haven't been taught how to read or write. So, lucky you!

Vanhessa smiled, this must be the girl's room, she deduced, and she took out her sword and sack, pushed the door open and went inside.

She did not find Rose but she did find a very startled guinea pig, his cheeks newly filled with lovely organic muesli.

Bubbles looked at the almighty warrior, a nut falling out of his open mouth. "Who the flipping heck are you?"

Vanhessa stared at Bubbles and licked her lips in a way he didn't at all like. It was a hungry look. He'd seen that look before on dogs' faces. Worse was to come as Bubbles spotted the necklace of dried rats.

I do not have to tell you that Bubbles promptly did a poo, even though he'd only done one three minutes earlier and wasn't due one for another four minutes.

Vanhessa leaned down to open the cage and avail herself of a snack when she heard the music stop in the room next door and a young boy's voice cry out, "Oh my god, you blooming thief!"

Kris had just realised his memory-wipe spell was missing! He stormed out of his room just as Vanhessa gave up on the idea of eating Bubbles and quickly hid inside the wardrobe.

Unaware there was a hulking great warrior with a broadsword hiding in the wardrobe, Kris blithely stomped into Rose's room and started to search for his spell.

"Kris, get out of here! Quickly!" Bubbles whisper-shouted frantically.

"Nice try, Bubbles, but I know she took the spell, so don't waste your breath."

"Kris, I'm serious. You've got to get out of here! GET OUT!" the guinea pig squeaked.

"Yeah, right. Nice try . . . Aha!" Kris had found the piece of paper that Rose had hidden in the bottom of the drawer – just as the door to the wardrobe creaked open and the giant sixth-century Vandal warrior crept silently out, exactly as she did when she went bear hunting.

Bubbles was beside himself with worry now. "She's going to KILL YOU, you idiot!"

Kris pouted and started searching under the bed. "She can try. I'm going to take some of *her* spells. See how she likes it."

"Stop, there's a—"

But before Bubbles could finish his sentence Kris turned to him with menace.

"And you're not going to tell her!" Kris snapped and then, in a move Bubbles did NOT see coming, read the memory-wipe spell . . .

"PRIMULA VERIS THINKSWIPEYMEMORALIS!"

he cried, throwing herbs in Bubbles's direction. Bubbles's eyes went blank again and he fell silent.

But Kris's glee was short-lived as Vanhessa, now right behind him, threw a sack over his head that came right down to his ankles.

Vanhessa trumpeted with joy. "And now I have you! Merdyn's going to be like a lamb to the slaughter!"

Kris hadn't got a clue what was happening, of course, so he just screamed loudly as Vanhessa tied the sack with some rope, flung it over her shoulder and ran out of the door, thwacking the flailing sack against the door frame on her way out.

In the silence that followed Bubbles came out of his spell trance.

"Huh? Hello? Anybody there?" But all seemed normal bar the open wardrobe doors and the dent in the door frame. "Weird." Bubbles shrugged and went back to his muesli.

*I wonder who opened
the wardrobe door?
Thought Bubbles, as a little poo
hit the floor.*

CHAPTER SIX

WORRIED MOTHERS AND MISSING BROTHERS

A few hours later, Rose and her mum arrived back from swimming to find the front door hanging off its hinges. They looked at each other for a split second before rushing into the house to find the sofa had been tipped over, the cupboards smashed, the fridge destroyed and the rib-eye steak stolen.

Mum called the police while Rose frantically ran upstairs to check Bubbles was OK. She found him still munching on muesli, as happy as can be.

"Bubbles, you're all right. Thank goodness! Do you know what happened?"

"Of course," he answered in his typically nonchalant way.

"Great. What? Tell me!" Rose implored.

"Well, I don't know the ins and outs but . . . the

wardrobe door came open."

Rose waited for more, but Bubbles carried on eating muesli.

"Is that it?" she said finally.

Bubbles stared back, confused. "What else do you want me to say?"

"So, you don't know what happened downstairs?"

"Why? What's happened downstairs?"

"The house has been destroyed. The sofa and chairs are tipped over. The fridge has been CUT IN TWO!"

"Has it?" Bubbles wrinkled his nose. "Huh. Didn't hear a thing."

At that moment Rose suddenly had a dreadful thought. Wasn't Kris here this afternoon? She rushed into his semi-destroyed room but Kris wasn't there. Although he'd evidently been organising his spells while doodling another stupid superhero outfit.

Rose went back into her room, plucked her mobile phone from its charger and called her brother. Since the war between them had begun she hadn't called him or texted him and she felt bad about this as she looked for his number "Kris bro mob".

She felt even worse when the call went straight to answerphone.

"Yo, whasuuuup. This is Kris aka Magiboy at your service. Leave me a message and I'll save your life later!" BEEP!

Rose was worried now. Had something happened to Kris?

She texted him.

ROSE
Kris u OK? Where r u? Worried.

She hesitated before putting an "X" on the end and sent it. After she pressed send, she saw a load of old exchanges between them, from around the time Merdyn had left.

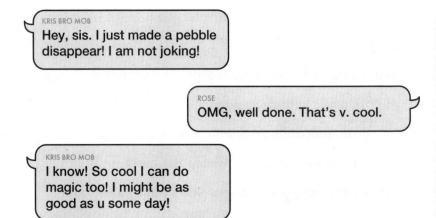

KRIS BRO MOB
Hey, sis. I just made a pebble disappear! I am not joking!

ROSE
OMG, well done. That's v. cool.

KRIS BRO MOB
I know! So cool I can do magic too! I might be as good as u some day!

Rose felt herself getting emotional. Her heart started to race. Her stomach went hot. Her eyes began to well up. She and Kris got on so well then. They'd both been so excited by this new life of theirs, about all the discoveries they could make and share together. How had it all gone so wrong? She blamed herself. She'd been so jealous that Kris had become better than her. Why? Why had she let that bother her? So what if he used his powers of invisibility to get into fashion shows for free? What did that matter? How foolish she'd been. She began to cry at the thought that something bad might have happened to him.

Rose went to get a tissue from her bedside table when something caught her eye on the floor. She picked it up. It was half Kris's memory-wipe spell, the one she had stolen from his room and hidden in her bottom drawer. But why was it now on the floor? And why was it torn in half?

"Do you know anything about this, Bubbles?"

"I do indeed," said Bubbles confidently.

Rose sighed in relief. "Oh thank god."

"That thing you're holding is called a *piece of paper*."

Rose flung her arms silently around in frustration.

Wow, having a talking guinea pig was annoying sometimes!

"Come on, Bubbles! Something weird happened here. Don't you remember anything?"

"I told you, the wardrobe door was shut one minute, and then it was open. That's all I know," said the guinea pig, offended by her tone of voice.

"Great! Very useful, thank you." Rose glanced towards the wardrobe and something else caught her eye, something rather more interesting than a piece of paper. For there, lying on the floor of the wardrobe, was a dried, perfectly preserved . . . *dead rat*.

Bubbles saw it too and was so shocked he stopped eating.

"What the actually, literally . . . is *that*?" he said. (Bubbles had started using more "youthful" language now that he'd been hanging out with Rose and Tamsin more, but he didn't actually know how to use the words properly.)

"I've seen a rat like this before somewhere," said Rose, and she started looking through her bookshelves.

"So have I!" Bubbles blurted fearfully, "In my literal, actual nightmares!!"

Then Rose found what she was looking for: a book called *Wizards, Witches and Warlocks of Auld*.

"When Merdyn was here he showed me this picture of his arch-enemy, the king of the Vandals." Rose explained to her VERY freaked-out guinea pig. "He wore a kind of tribal necklace with tiger teeth on it and—"

"Don't tell me. Let me guess!" Bubbles interrupted. "Erm . . . dried dead rats?"

Rose found the picture of Vanheldon she'd been looking for and, sure enough, there it was, the same dried dead rat hanging on a piece of leather round his neck.

Rose's mind was completely blown. OK. So she had made a connection between a dead rat in her bedroom and a warlord from AD 500. But how would that help anyone? What was the dried rat doing here? In the twenty-first century? It couldn't possibly belong to Vanheldon, could it? She looked at her phone. No text from Kris. Where WAS he? Rose was flummoxed with a capital F.

Bubbles, meanwhile, was having a nervous breakdown. He was simultaneously terrified and saddened by the dead rat. It looked pathetic, its eyes popping out of its head and its tail shrivelled like a worm that had been in the sun for days.

"I mean, I'm not a fan of rats," Bubbles said, sniffing, "but they are fellow rodents after all. Look at him. Or *her*," he said, correcting himself; he didn't want to sound sexist. "Taken in the prime of its life. It can't have been more than a year old. Goodness knows what brothers or sisters it left behind!" Then Bubbles started to cry at his own eulogy.

But as Bubbles blubbed, a light bulb went off in Rose's brain.

"That's it, Bubbles!"

Bubbles was rightly confused. "What's it?"

"We need to find out how old this thing is."

"It's not a *thing*, Rose! It has a name, you know!" wailed a now over-emotional Bubbles as Rose picked him up and ran down the stairs.

She bumped into her distraught mother on her way out of the door.

"Where you off to?"

"I'm, er . . . just going to try to find Kris. He's not answering his phone."

"I know. I've been trying him too. OK. Well, don't you go disappearing as well! Sergeant Murray's on his way."

Rose disappeared and Suzy looked at her wrecked house.

"Gosh, how much worse can this day get?"

Oh, Suzy, you ain't seen nothing yet ...

CHAPTER SEVEN

TIME-TRAVEL TRICKS
AND
HEADS ON STICKS

If you thought your last holiday to Spain with your family was an ordeal, you should try Kris's journey to Dark Ages Transylvania. First he was dragged, sometimes literally, the 1,300 miles or so from Bashingford to Romania. Then he was pulled through the Rivers of Time, which is quite an ordeal in and of itself. And all this while he was encased in a hessian sack with no mirror or hair product!

It was safe to say that Kris was terrified. Where the heck was this unreasonably strong woman taking him to? When would they get there? What or who would be there when they arrived? What did they want from him? And what did his hair look like?

He had occasionally tried to talk to his captor, even joking by asking "Are we there yet?" on occasions, but Vanhessa had been told by her father not to say a word to the prisoner, and she was nothing if not a good warrior and obeyed.

Along the journey Kris had managed to poke a tiny hole through the sack and what he saw confused him greatly. First of all there were no buildings ANYWHERE! Just endless trees, tall grass, rivers and valleys. And there were no PEOPLE either – just the odd deer, horse and huge birds that circled the skies in their thousands. Where was everybody?

Eventually he heard Vanhessa knock on what sounded like a large wooden door, and when Kris looked out of his little peephole he was nearly sick to his completely empty stomach. For up on the wall in front of him, stuck on sharpened stakes, were the severed heads of DEAD ANIMALS! Pigs, goats, bears, a wolf. Bleurgh!! Kris retched in his sack.

"Quiet!" came the order from his captor.

The next thing Kris heard was the huge double gate of Fort Doom opening and he was carried inside. *I don't know what this place is, but who in their right mind would decorate their front gate with decapitated heads?!* thought Kris. *Only someone who loved killing and didn't mind who knew it, that's who!* he concluded, which was, of course, the desired effect of said dead heads.

A few minutes later, in the courtyard, Vanhessa stood proudly before her father and Druilla. She could barely believe that her mission had been successful. To travel forward in time, kidnap a child and bring them back in time again!? That took some doing. But she'd done it.

"Behold," said Vanhessa with great fanfare. "Merdyn's beloved descendant, Rose." She opened up the wriggling sack and Kris spilled out, blinking at the sunlight in the old fort's courtyard.

He immediately stood upright, which was difficult as his hands were tied behind his back. His eyes darted wildly around before landing on the strangest figures he'd ever seen – and he'd met Merdyn the Wild!

First there was the man mountain Vanheldon with his face that looked like a massive shovel had sprouted a beard. He looked like one of those shouty American wrestlers that he used to watch with his dad. This one would be called The Human Mountain. Then there was the dark haunting old lady witch with a stick. Her piercing blue eyes were enough to spook you alone.

"A-all right," Kris stammered finally. "Who are you? Where am I?"

Vanheldon looked at Kris. His tight skinny jeans. His black sneakers with the laces undone. His blue T-shirt with holes in. And his weird standy-up hair (Kris's hairspray was still doing a good job even now). The ex-Vandal king marched up to Kris, grabbed his face and inspected him more closely. Kris retched again at the smell emanating from Vanheldon's mouth*. It was disgusting, like a cross between rotting meat and gone-off eggs.

"This is not a girl," Vanheldon concluded of his inspection of Kris. "It's a boy."

"Is it?" said Vanhessa, peering at him and also breathing her stinky breath on him.

Kris was about to faint with the mixture of disorientation, severed heads on sticks and rotten meat/ eggy breath.

The witch muttered a few words while waving her

----

*Remember there was no toothpaste in the Dark Ages (it wouldn't be invented until the 1800s) and the most they ever used to do was poke in between their teeth with sticks. So remember how lucky you are next time you moan about brushing your teeth before school!

fingers about, and suddenly Kris could understand the conversation. "Thou art right. It is not Rose," spoke Druilla. "The stories say she is red of hair, freckled of face and has glass eye-shields* that sit atop her nose in an iron cradle."

"Rose?" Kris perked up at the mention of his sister's name. "This has something to do with my sister?" He was hoping Rose might be here – as much as they had been fighting recently what he wouldn't have given to have seen his little sister right then!

"Thou art a fool, Vanhessa!!" bellowed Vanheldon at his poor daughter. "Why did all my sons have to die in battle and leaveth me with THEE?!!"

Vanhessa felt like crying, but it was definitely not very warrior-like to start crying. It's the first thing they teach you at warrior school: absolutely no blubbing!

"I am sorry, Father. I have letteth thee down." She hung her head.

"Yes thou have!" barked her father cruelly. "Well,

---

*Although the Romans experimented with blown glass to magnify text (effectively making a magnifying glass), the first wearable glasses wouldn't be invented until the thirteenth century (in Italy). If you were short-sighted before then you just had to lump it. So think about that the next time you visit the opticians!

don't just stand there. Killeth the boy and put his head upon a stake. We have no need for him now."

"Yes, Father," said Vanhessa, and obediently unsheathed her broadsword.

Kris's heart pounded in his chest like a blindfolded boxer in a panic room.

"Whoa, whoa, hey now!" he said, quaking. "Let's just think about this for a second." He was trying to buy time. Surely he couldn't just die now, right? After being kidnapped and dragged around in a sack for two weeks, he was going to be killed and his head put on a stake just like that!? He hadn't even checked his hair! And why was he being killed? For NOT being his sister? Weirdest. Day. Ever!

Even Vanhessa thought it was a waste too. All that time-travelling, all that trekking? But . . . she must obey her father's wishes and that was that. She raised her sword above Kris's neck. She pulled the sword back and swung with all her might.

"Wait!!"

Vanhessa's sword stopped inches from Kris's neck.

Kris let out a thankful whimper. His saviour was Druilla.

"If he is the brother of Rose, then he is also Merdyn's descendant. He could yet be useful . . ."

Druilla reached into her dark, dirty cloak and pulled out a crystal ball. She held it with one hand and rubbed it with the other, staring deeply into its depths.

Vanhessa and Vanheldon looked at each other. What was she up to now?

"Ah yes. Yes, yes, yes, yes, yes," Druilla muttered, smiling in a terrifying way. "This is all very good for us. The crystal ball has shown me. Rose will cometh. From the future."

Kris roused himself from his "thankful to be alive" mindset and entered the "say what now" realm of thinking.

"Excuse me. Sorry. The future? So, like, am I in the past? Is that why there's no houses and stuff here? Wait. What year is this?"

"'Tis 521," Vanhessa informed him, which made Kris feel very faint again.

"You have GOT to be kidding me!" he cried.

Druilla was still peering into the crystal ball. "Yeees! And she will bring Merdyn the Wild. And finally the powers of darkness will defeateth the insipid power of light! Yeees, the crystal ball telleth me all." And she cackled in the way that evil people often do. "The light? The light cometh to me. Can thou see it?"

Then, all of a sudden, strange particles of light appeared from nowhere and started floating towards Druilla's fingers. She dropped her walking stick and stood upright, like she had de-aged ten years in five seconds. Kris and the Vandals' mouths fell open like trouts gasping for air.

"Do thou see? It is working. The light maketh me stronger," she rejoiced, and then, with a more menacing look in her eye added, "And after light cometh ... *darkness*!!"

And she thrust her hands to the sky, sending black tendrils from her fingers streaming up into the clouds.

Down below the forest, in the local village, a market was in full flow. A flower seller and her customer both saw black tendrils rising up from the forest on the hillside.

The flower seller sighed. "Looks like an evil sorceress

just moved in."

The customer nodded wearily and said, "Yeah, looks that way dunnit," before handing over his money and walking gloomily off.

> *Oh, villagers, do not go gentle*
> *into that dark night.*
> *Fight, fight against the dying*
> *of the light!*

CHAPTER EIGHT

'A RAT DISMEMBERED AND A GUINEA PIG REMEMBERS

Now I know my readers are very clever. I don't need to tell you what carbon dating is, do I? No, it's not two people called Carbon going for dinner to get to know each other better. No, no. Carbon dating is a scientific way of finding out how old things are.

As soon as Rose left the house with her dead rat and her alive guinea pig she headed to see her friend and co-worker at her vet clinic, Tamsin. Tamsin's mum worked in a lab at the university, and it just so happened she had access to a carbon-dating machine.

Tamsin cut the rat in half and took some tissue from its insides. Then she slid the sample into the machine. A short time later, Tamsin saw the result on the computer screen.

"Rose . . ." Tamsin trembled breathlessly. "This rat died 1,500 years ago. The year 521 to be precise."

The blood drained from Rose's face. "So . . ." Rose began piecing the evidence together like a detective on a TV show. "Someone came from the Dark Ages. Someone bad and . . . and . . ."

"And what?" asked Tamsin.

Rose's similarity to a TV detective was crumbling already. "That's just it. I don't know . . ."

"Put Kris in a sack and took him away," said Bubbles from Rose's pocket.

"WHAT?!" Rose and Tamsin exclaimed simultaneously.

"I SAID THEY PUT KRIS IN A SACK AND TOOK HIM AWAY! Yeah. Big woman. Very strong. Stinky. She was hiding in the wardrobe." He then found a piece of muesli at the bottom of Rose's pocket and began chewing on it nonchalantly.

Rose had been annoyed with Bubbles before but now she was fuming. "Why didn't you say this before?!"

"I've only just remembered!" Bubbles complained.

"Kris put a spell on me and I forgot everything."

Rose sighed. "Ah, of course!"

Tamsin was thoroughly confused. "What is going on?"

"Kris made a memory-wipe spell," explained Rose. "It must have worn off so Bubbles is getting his memory back." She looked at Bubbles. "Do you remember anything else?"

"Erm . . . I remember you stole it from him in the first place," said Bubbles.

"Tamsin doesn't need to hear that!" Rose muttered guiltily, trying to quickly move on. "What else do you remember? Did she say anything, this strong woman?"

"She spoke in a foreign language, maybe German? So it was hard to understand but it sounded to me something like 'And now I have you! Merdyn's going to be like a lamb to the slaughter!'"

The final piece of the jigsaw clicked into place and Rose reverted to detective mode, this time a bit more successfully.

"It's Vanheldon. It must be. He's setting some sort of

trap for Merdyn. He sent someone to take Kris." Secretly Rose was a bit upset that he hadn't sent someone to kidnap *her*. It was a silly thought, but she couldn't help it. She supposed that Kris was better than her at magic and maybe that made him more valuable. She shook herself out of these thoughts. *Stop feeling sorry for yourself, Rose!* she told herself.

Rose thanked Tamsin and raced out of the lab.

"May I ask where we're going?" asked Bubbles as he bounced about in her pocket, his cheeks full of muesli.

"Home to get my spellbook. And then we're going to the Dark Ages."

Bubbles spat the muesli out. "PWAAAAT?!" (Which is not something he would ever dream of doing unless he was in deep shock.)

He looked up at Rose, terrified. "Have you gone totally crazy in the coconut?! Have you *seen* what they do to rodents in the Dark Ages?!"

But Rose wasn't ready to listen.
On her mind was an important mission.

CHAPTER NINE

NEWS OF DARK AGES, RAGES, AND PANIC STAGES!

Meanwhile, in Daffodil Close, Mum was in the kitchen with Sergeant Murray and Dion, her boyfriend.

Sergeant Murray had the whole thing sussed. "Oh yes, this is a classic robbery," he said.

"But . . . all they took was a rib-eye steak," Dion remarked. He'd been *really* looking forward to that steak.

"It wasn't a robbery!" Rose blurted as she burst into the kitchen.

"What was it then?" asked the policeman.

"It was a kidnap."

"For it to be a kidnap there has to be a missing person," protested Sergeant Murray.

"There is," said Rose. "Kris."

"Kris?!" Mum was already starting to panic. "What are you talking about? What's happened?"

Rose took a deep breath, then let it out. "Kris has been taken back to the Dark Ages by Merdyn's enemy."

"WHAT?!" Mum's panic was now in full flow. "Why would they do that?"

"I don't know," Rose said. "I think they're using Kris to trap Merdyn."

"So he's BAIT?" Mum was beyond panic now and was entering the realm of hysterical. "He's being used as BAIT to lure Merdyn? My little boy?! A worm on a hook?!"

Mum's eyes were as big as cartwheels and her hands began to shake. Dion had to help her into a chair.

"Just breathe, love," Dion soothed. "In, out, in, out."

Mum caught her breath and tried to think. She hoped that Rose had got this all wrong, but she'd learned a long time ago that no matter how ludicrous Rose sounded, what she said was probably true. She hadn't believed Rose when she'd told her that a wizard from the Dark Ages was living in their shed, so why doubt that her son had been kidnapped and taken back in time?

Sergeant Murray knew not to doubt Rose too. "Well, I'm afraid the Dark Ages are out of my jurisdiction. I do cover crimes in Bashingford but only present-day ones. I'll leave this in your capable hands, young Rose." And with that he hotfooted it out of the house.

"OK," Mum said at last, Dion's breathing technique having brought her back from hysterical to just plain panic. "So what do we do?"

"Well, I've been thinking about that," Rose said.

"She wants to go back in time and rescue him," Bubbles piped up from Rose's pocket.

"WHAT?!" Mum was back in hysterical mode. "Are you OUT OF YOUR MIND?!"

"That's literally what I said!" Bubbles enthused. "Except I said 'Have you gone totally crazy in the coconut?' so not literally, literally, but close."

"But, Mum, what choice do we have? We can't just leave him there," Rose said.

Suzy knew Rose was right, but she was now crossing over to the angry zone.

"Stupid Merdyn the Wild!" she fumed. "Even when he's not here he's causing trouble. All right. How do we go back in time?"

Rose hesitated. "Well, *I* will go back using Jerabo's spellbook*." she said. "I'll perform the Rivers of Time spell, find Merdyn and together we'll go and rescue Kris, wherever he is."

"If you think you're going on your own, you are sorely mistaken, my girl," Mum replied rather forcefully.

"Mum, you can't come."

"Why not?"

"Because it could be dangerous."

"That's why I've got to go!"

"But, Mum, you're not a W-blood. I am."

"You can be blue blood for all I care. What if you don't come back? I can't have TWO children in the Dark Ages! I'm coming with you whether you like it or not!"

Dion thought he'd better interject. He'd only just found Suzy, he didn't want to lose her in a weird time loop. "Listen, love, what if Rose is right? If you don't have magic blood or whatever . . . "

---

*This spellbook was how Merdyn was sent forward in time in the first place. Jerabo was jealous of Merdyn, so sent him into the Rivers of Time. Years later, Jerabo's descendant, Julian Smith, found his dusty spellbook in an attic. After Merdyn returned home Julian gave the book to Rose as it was useless to him because Merdyn had taken away Julian's magic powers as punishment for helping his ancestor to try to take over the world. All make sense? Good. I'm glad somebody knows what's going on . . .

"W-blood," Rose reminded him.

"W-blood, right." Then Dion continued. "I mean, what if you, like, spontaneously combusted or disintegrated or . . . or worse?"

"What could be worse than those?" Bubbles asked unhelpfully as ever.

But Suzy was not for turning. "My son has been kidnapped! I can't just sit here and do nothing. I don't care about the risks. It's a mother's instinct to protect her children. I'd do the same for you, Rose. I'm sorry, but I'm coming with you whether you like it or not."

Dion looked crestfallen. Rose hung her head too. Then she had an idea.

"OK, Mum. You can come with me."

"Good!" Mum said, relieved the argument was over.

Dion shot Rose a worried glance

but Rose widened her eyes as if to say, "Just go along with me." "But, er . . . the Rivers of Time? Merdyn told me they could get pretty cold, and wet. So you'd best pack some clothes and maybe get us both some waterproofs."

"Right, yeah, that figures. I'll go and get ready," Mum said and rushed upstairs.

When she was gone Dion shot Rose that glance again. "Rose, she can't go."

"I know," said Rose quickly. "That's why you're going to cover for me. While Mum gets her stuff I'm going to grab my spellbook and go. Mum'll be cross but I've got to go alone. I'll be back with Kris as soon as I can."

"OK," said Dion a little nervously.

Rose quietly skipped upstairs and grabbed her spellbook while being careful not to alert Mum who was rifling through her wardrobe. Rose grabbed her blue denim jacket just in case it *was* a bit cold in the Rivers, and Bubbles grabbed his Dictaphone so he could keep up with his diary. Then Rose popped her pet and his recording device in her jacket pocket and they rushed downstairs.

Dion met Rose at the front door and as he was a film

buff he gave Rose a bit of advice on time travel that he'd picked up from time-travel films like *Back to the Future*. "Don't change anything, no matter how small, because it'll have a knock-on effect over time. If you tell someone how a car engine works, for example, you'll get back to the future and everyone'll be driving around in, like, really advanced cars that fly and stuff."

"Well, luckily I don't know how engines work," said Rose.

"I do," said Bubbles.

Rose ignored him. "Wish me luck," she said, and raced out of the front door.

On the road outside her house Rose opened the spellbook to the Rivers of Time page.

"Is it right what you said about the Rivers of Time?" Bubbles asked her. "Will it be cold and wet?"

But Rose had no time to think about that. Any second now Mum would find out she was gone and run out of the house trying to stop her.

She looked for the herb required to make the spell work. Of course it was thyme – pretty obvious when you think about it. Rose was nervous. She'd only ever seen Merdyn perform the Rivers of Time spell and he was the greatest wizard who ever lived. She only hoped she could achieve such a mighty feat of magic – but she had to. And quickly.

There was no time to lose. She read the spell aloud:

"BARBARIS, REVENTIUM CLOCKASHOCK!"

and green light shone from a hole in the tarmac in front of her. A thrill ran through her – she'd done it!

Meanwhile, inside the house, Suzy ran back down the stairs with two raincoats and some sweaters.

"All right, we're ready . . . What the— Where's Rose?" she asked Dion.

"Erm, well, she, er . . ." Dion stuttered.

Through the window Suzy could see Rose in the street, a green light before her.

Suzy knew that light! "Is my daughter going back in time without me?" she exclaimed before dumping the coats and sweaters and tearing out of the door.

A second later, she raced outside just in time to see the light disappear and the ground close up. Suzy knelt where the hole had been, now solid road again. A faint whisp of magical smoke hung in the air.

She banged her fist on the tarmac. "Rose!!" She banged again. "Rose!!" She looked up to the heavens then. "Noooooooooo!"

Dion came out and put his arm round the sobbing Suzy and walked her inside.

The neighbours all looked out of their windows, curtains twitching.

"Never a dull moment in that house," an old lady said to her sleepy cat.

One child lost in time
was a scandal.
To lose another
was too much to handle!

CHAPTER TEN

A SPELL SUBLIME
AND THE
RIVERS OF TIME

The joy at having successfully performed such an awesome spell was cut short when Rose faced the bizarre reality of the Rivers of Time itself. It was not at all as Rose or Bubbles had imagined it. It was neither wet nor dry, loud nor quiet, bright nor dark. It defied categorisation. It was like it existed between everything – always there but not visible, like the insulation foam between the walls of your house. Didn't know you had insulation foam between the walls of your house? Then I have proved my point.

Rose thought it was a little like being on a roller coaster in a black hole in space. Fast but windless. Bubbles didn't care to even think about describing it; he just wanted it to end! But where, or more to the point *when*, would it end? Would they be stuck in there for ever?

Then Rose noticed that little tunnels kept appearing

here and there. They would appear for a few seconds, showing themselves as a wispy grey shadow, then disappear in a flash. She figured these must be time holes, little streams that run off the main river. Ways out perhaps. But which one should she choose? She thought about the year she needed to arrive at. And as soon as she thought "521" she and Bubbles veered sideways with great force, as if being hit by a bumper car – THUMP – into one of the wispy grey side tunnels.

They flew along at a windless high speed as before, but this time Rose could see the edges of a tunnel, like the walls of a cave. She thought again: 521. WHOOSH! She and Bubbles were pummelled from the side, even harder this time, into a thinner tunnel.

"Make it STOP!" shrieked Bubbles, before pressing record on his Dictaphone. "Note to self: time travel is NOT FUN!"

Rose thought again, even harder this time. She closed her eyes and concentrated on three shapes: 5 2 1. WHUMP, WHUMP, WHUMP – they were buffeted from tunnel to tunnel, but now they could hear a noise, like the engine of a jumbo jet roaring. Rose saw a light up ahead, a small narrow light – the black space splitting just a smidge – then the screeching became louder and louder and the split in the dark fabric got closer and closer. SCREEEEECH.

"AAAAAARGH! I HAAAAATE THIS MORE THAN DOOOOGS!"

Then the pair were blinded by an intense light and the screeching stopped. As Rose's eyes adjusted, she found herself . . . in a beautiful field of daffodils. She'd made it! She'd actually travelled back in time. Rescuing Kris alive and well was obviously the main thing but she couldn't help but wonder how impressed he'd be when he realised she'd managed to nail one of the most spectacular spells there is!

Rose allowed herself a BIG a sigh of relief, then looked up at the sky. It was a bright azure blue. She couldn't remember a time when she'd seen anything bluer. The sun was different too, somehow larger and yellower than she'd seen it before. Even the air was different. It smelled incredible. Like fresh laundry times a million.

As Rose breathed it in and out of her lungs it almost felt nourishing*.

She took Bubbles out of her backpack. He still had his eyes firmly closed.

"Bubbles, look at the Dark Ages. It's beautiful."

"I absolutely refuse to open my eyes ever again after what you just put me through," rasped Bubbles angrily. "Did you even ask me if I wanted to go back in time? I don't think you did." Then he spoke into his Dictaphone. "Note to self: tell Rose to ask me first if I ever want to do ANYTHING EVER!"

"Shut up and open your eyes," Rose demanded. She gave him a shake until he opened his eyes.

He looked around. "Hmm. Not bad, I suppose," he said, trying not to be impressed by the thirty acres of daffodils waving in the bright sunshine. "Who's he, though?" asked Bubbles, nodding to the side.

Rose turned and saw a man staring at them. He wore dirty clothes and was pushing a pig in a small wooden cage on wheels. Rose thought he looked like he was from about

----

*Remember, not only were there no cars, lorries and planes in the Dark Ages, there were no factories, no power stations or as many people. The air was as pure as nature intended it, bar the odd animal trump.

the right time period. He must be a peasant taking his pig to market. He was staring at them with his mouth wide open, a piece of hay dangling precariously from his bottom lip.

"What year be-eth this, kind sir?" Rose asked, using the ye-oldy-est-sounding language she could muster.

"I dunno, do I?" came the short, rather unexpected answer.**

"Does thou knowest a wizard called Merdyn?" Rose asked.

"Merdyn?!" cried the man as if he knew him.

"Yes, Merdyn. Do you know him?"

"Nope," came another rather short and unexpected reply.

Rose's heart sank. Merdyn had said a thousand times that everybody in his time knew him. She must have gone too far back in time. Or not far enough. But she was sure she'd steered herself to the year 521.

"Are you certain?" she tried again. "He's tall, has a"

** Most people in the Dark Ages would have had no idea what year it was; things like that were for the nobility and church folk. A peasant like this gentleman would have known lots about calendar events and festivities (of which there were many throughout the year) but he wouldn't have been able to tell you the year or probably even how old he was. I wish I lived in the Dark Ages sometimes, then I could pretend I was twenty-one again year after year!

long dark beard, wears purple robes. Kind of arrogant but charming."

"Nope," said the man again. "Oh, hang on . . ." The man perked up, giving Rose hope once more. "Did you say Merdyn?"

Rose cheered. "Yes! Merdyn the Wild. So you know him?"

"Nooo."

Rose gave up. Her time in the Dark Ages was going to be difficult if everyone was as stupid as this bloke.

"I know a *Merlin*, though," the annoying man said calmly. "Merlin the Great."

Rose slapped her forehead. Of course! Merdyn had gone back in time and become Merlin. It wasn't this man with a pig who was stupid; it was Rose!

"Yes, that's him," she said rather bashfully. "Great. It must be the year 521. Do you know where he is?"

"He'll be at the magic circle. It's that way as the crow flies*." The man pointed into the distance. "It's summer solstice** today."

----

*This is a term (still used today) that means "in a straight line", like a crow flies, although I have seen crows going around in circles, so I'm not sure this saying stands up to too much scrutiny.

"Thank you so much, good peasant," said Rose, bowing her head and heading off in the direction the man had pointed.

"Who's she calling a peasant? Cheeky cow," said the man to the pig.

The pig grunted back as if to say it couldn't agree more.

The man lifted his wheelbarrow after Rose had gone.
"Huh," he said to himself.
"I did not know it was 521!"

**Summer solstice or the midsummer festival is celebrated when the sun is at its highest, meaning more daylight hours. It is sometimes called "the longest day". It is thought that Stonehenge was designed with the solstice in mind. On this day when the sun rises its rays shine through a tiny gap in the Heel Stone, the main entrance to the stone circle. To this day hundreds of people still gather at Stonehenge to watch this ancient spectacle.

CHAPTER ELEVEN

PREPARE TO BE EXCITED AS TWO OLD PALS ARE REUNITED

It was a long walk to the magic circle, or Stonehenge to you and me. But Rose had been there before and pretty much knew the way. Although there were no roads or buildings, of course. There was LOTS of wildlife, though. There were butterflies and birds and rabbits and hares and deer at every turn. The grass was tall and abundant and waterways criss-crossed the land*. *Earth really does belong to nature*, thought Rose.

Bubbles had been pretty quiet along the way, but he eventually piped up. "Can I have some muesli please? I'm starving."

Rose suddenly felt guilty. In the rush to get out of the house she'd completely forgotten to pack any of Bubbles's

----

*Britain used to have many, many more rivers and streams in the Dark Ages. Years of farming and the construction of towns and villages have seen rivers diverted and even forced underground. In north London, for example, Fleet Road is named after the river that used to flow there and which now runs UNDERNEATH the road. So check it out — you might be sitting above an ancient river as you read!!

beloved organic muesli.

"Sorry, Bubbles. I forgot to grab your food."

"What the literally actual actually literally flipping heck?!" shrieked Bubbles.

"I'm sorry, OK? I was in a rush."

"Oh, in a rush, were you? You managed to grab your stupid spellbook, though?"

"I needed that to get back in time in the first place. Kris's life is in danger. We're here to rescue him, remember! I'm bound to prioritise the spellbook over your muesli!"

Bubbles was furious and he wanted Rose to know it, so he pressed record on his Dictaphone again. "Note to self: get a new owner that cares about me."

Rose wasn't going to take this lying down. "Hang on, YOU managed to grab your stupid Dictaphone, so why didn't YOU grab some food? Or at least remind me to grab it."

Bubbles twitched his whiskers, irritated. Damn! She'd got him there. Not that he was going to let Rose know it.

"That's very insensitive, Rose. I need that recording

device for my disability."

Rose looked confused. "What disability?"

"My terrible memory," said Bubbles. "I tend to forget all the great thoughts I have, but with my Dictaphone they are there for ever. Or at least you write them down and I have myself a bestselling book."

"OK, Bubbles," Rose relented, "whatever you say."

"We're going to have to visit a pet shop then," Bubbles added. "There must be one around here somewhere?"

"Erm, this is the Dark Ages, Bubbles. There're no pet shops here."

"What??!" cried Bubbles, apoplectic with rage. "Then what am I supposed to eat?"

Rose gazed around her. "Look at all this vegetation. You used to love grass and carrots and stuff."

"But that was before I knew better!" huffed Bubbles. "Once you've tasted organic muesli, there's no turning back. It's your fault . . ."

"*My* fault? Why's it my fault?"

"Because you bought me the organic muesli . . ."

And so another argument started up. But we'll leave

Rose and Bubbles arguing for now, shall we, and leap towards their destination. Stonehenge . . .

At Stonehenge a crowd was gathered for the summer solstice. Merdyn was making a speech to a crowd of two or three hundred people. He was ten years older than when we last saw him. He had aged well; his hair and beard were longer and speckled with grey. He was certainly wiser and kinder than when we last met him (thanks to Rose showing him it's best to use magic powers for good not mischief) but his eye belied a sense of mischief still.

By his side was his wife Evanhart, with her silver-grey eyes, long red hair and freckles. And by her side were two children. A red-haired girl, aged nine, and a cheeky-looking six-year-old boy who was the spitting image of Merdyn (but without the beard). Next to Evanhart stood Merdyn's very dignified-looking pet wolf, imaginatively called Wolf.

Next to Evanhart, sitting on an ornate throne, was the

new king of England. At first glance you might think he was a pretty normal-looking king; he wore kingly robes and had a crown on top of his head, but look a little closer and you would see that he was smaller than a normal-sized man and had not a trace of facial hair. This is because the king was twelve years old. His name was King Arthur, aka the boy king. Perhaps you've heard of him*?

Merdyn was in the middle of his speech and had the crowd enraptured. He was giving thanks, as he did every year, for all the things that we have to be grateful for. The earth, the sky, the wind, the sun, the moon, the rain. For nature and for friends and family. Not just the ones we're here with today but those from our past and those in our future. Then, as he did every year, he gave thanks to Rose.

"She taughteth me what was right from what was wrong; she had wisdom beyond her years. I know many of ye have heardeth the stories of my journey to the future. It

----

*Legend has it that when the previous king died without a male heir a stone appeared with a sword in it. It was decreed that whoever could pull the sword from the stone was the rightful heir to the throne. Several burly knights and general tough guys tried and failed until one day a scrawny kid called Arthur pulled it out easily. As a side note to this footnote, twelve is not very young for a king. The youngest king of England is Henry the Sixth who succeeded to the throne in 1421 aged eight months and twenty-six days!

was ten years ago now, but I still thinketh about Rose and what she meant to me almost every day."

Coincidentally, just at that moment, Merdyn heard the faintest shout of his name.

"Merdyn!" came the faint cry.

Merdyn smiled. "Sometimes I can almost hear her call my name. She calls me 'Merdyn'."

"Merdyn, it's me!"

Merdyn smiled again. "I can almost hear her shouting 'Merdyn, it's me!'."

"Merdyn!"

"There it is again," said Merdyn, grinning ruefully and gazing into the sky.

But behind him Evanhart and Wolf were looking at each other. They could hear someone shouting too.

Then Merdyn looked down to see the image of Rose, dressed in her modern garb and carrying her faithful guinea pig through the field of wild grass outside the henge.

He literally couldn't believe his eyes. "Sometimes I even thinketh I see her," Merdyn said to the crowd. "I see her running towards me, her silly guinea pig in her arms, calling 'Merdyn, it's me!'."

Wolf had pretty good eyesight, plus he could talk, courtesy of a pinecone spell, and so he bounded up to Merdyn and said, "Forgive me, sire, but I thinketh that IS a young girl coming towards thee."

Merdyn squinted. "But it can't be . . . Rose? Here?

No . . ."

When Rose entered the stone circle the Dark Ages crowd parted at the sight of this strangely dressed little girl and her pet.

"Rose!" cried Merdyn and ran to embrace her.

Neither Rose nor Merdyn had ever dreamed they would see each other again. They embraced with all their might!

"Merdyn, listen . . ." Rose started, meaning to tell him that her reason for being here was not a cheery one. But Merdyn was too excited to listen. There were so many people he wanted Rose to meet.

"This is Evanhart!" he said, bringing the two freckly redheads together.

Evanhart and Rose laughed. It was clear they were related.

"Greetings, Rose," said Evanhart, hugging her. "I've heard so much about thee."

"This is Lily and Gulliver, my children," Merdyn said excitedly, then turned to the children and pointed at Rose. "This is thy great great great great great great great great

great great great too many greats to mention grandchild. Well, I don't know which of ye she descendeth from. Can ye believe it?"

"No," said Gulliver, causing all to laugh.

Lily looked shyly at Rose and hid behind Evanhart's legs.

"Rose, this is King Arthur," said Merdyn, and Arthur now stepped forward, taking Rose's hand and kissing it.

"I have never seeneth such beauty, not even in the heavens themselves," he said, completely surprising Rose.

"O . . . K," she said slowly, then didn't know what to say so just said "Thanks".

Merdyn then turned to the rather frightening-looking wolf. He had sharp bright white teeth, yellow eyes and a shiny grey coat of hair with a white diamond shape on his chest. "This is my trusty canine guardian, Wolf," he said, and Wolf politely held a paw in the air that Rose shook.

"An honour to meet thee, Rose, I have certainly heard a lot about thee. All of it positive, I must say." He spoke as calmly and serenely as a well-trained butler. What followed, seconds later, was not very graceful, however, when Wolf caught sight of Bubbles. "GGGGGRRRRRat!!" he growled and went into a frenzy of snapping teeth and gnashing fangs.

"Whoa, whoa, stop, Wolf!" shouted Merdyn. "This is Bubbles, Rose's pet guinea pig."

"Ah. My apologies," said Wolf, calming down and composing himself. "I must say I have never heard of anyone keeping a *rodent* as a pet."

Bubbles felt extremely insulted. "Well, I've never heard of anyone having a vicious wolf as a pet so . . . that makes two of us, eh?" Then he turned quietly to his Dictaphone and pressed record. "Note to self: found something I hate more than dogs. Wolves."

Rose had more important things on her mind. "So nice to meet you all," she said, "but there's a reason I'm here and it's not a good one. Can we talk?"

"Of course, to the camp. We will have supper now. Come," said Merdyn. As they walked away the two relatives started chatting.

From Rose's pocket Bubbles eyeballed Wolf

as he walked by Merdyn's side. The wolf leaned towards Bubbles.

> *"I could eat thee*
> *in just one bite."*
> *"Go ahead and try.*
> *You'll be in for a fight."*

CHAPTER TWELVE

A QUESTION IS BEGGED
AND A
A MESSAGE IS PEGGED

Evanhart and Merdyn's children served food round the campfire as Rose filled Merdyn in on the events that had brought her back in time. Merdyn stared in disbelief at the two halves of the dried rat Rose had found in her bedroom.

"This belongs to the Vanheldon family all right," he deduced. "Though I doubt Vanheldon himself would have braved the Rivers of Time. They are not for the faint-hearted."

"Tell me about it!" Bubbles piped up. "I've haven't been right since."

"And Vanheldon isn't W-blood, right? They can't travel through the Rivers of Time anyway," Rose said, thinking of the excuse she'd given for leaving Mum behind.

"Oh, they can," said Merdyn. "As long as they have a W-blood to send them, of course."

Rose felt bad about Mum but surely she was better off out of this? Or was it that Rose had wanted to rescue Kris herself to prove that she was better than him at magic? She shook these thoughts from her mind and tuned back in to what Merdyn was saying.

"Vanheldon most likely sendeth his daughter, coward that he really is," the great wizard guessed (correctly!). "But the question remaineth: who is the W-blood that sendeth her?"

"And where is the message telling us he has Kris?" wondered Evanhart. "What if Rose had not cometh to tell us? We would never even have known of this travesty."

"Very good point, my darling," Merdyn agreed. "I suspect a message will be forthcoming."

Right on queue a raven fell out of the sky and landed next to the fire. As soon as it hit the ground the giant black bird breathed its last breath and died.

Merdyn unpicked a note that had been pegged to the raven's leg.

Bubbles stared at the poor dead bird. "What is it with these people and killing animals?"

"It is nature's way," Wolf growled at Bubbles with a raised doggy eyebrow.

Merdyn read the note out loud.

> MERDYN THE WILD, I HAVE THY GREAT GREAT GREAT GREAT GREAT GREAT GREAT GREAT GREAT GREAT GREAT GREAT GREAT GREAT GREAT—

he turned the page over and carried on –

> GREAT GREAT ET CETERA GRANDSON, KRIS. COME AND GETTETH HIM IF THOU DARE! IF THOU DO NOT, HE WILL DIE A DOZEN MOONS FROM NOW. LOVE AND KISSES, VANHELDON.

Everybody took in the grave news. Rose held her head in her hands. Twelve days to walk to Romania?!

But Merdyn was already up on his feet gathering his things, including Thundarian, his trusty wooden staff. Thundarian was a wonderfully gnarled piece of wood as tall as Merdyn's shoulders, with a proud eagle carved into its top end.

Evanhart shook her head as she reread the note.

"Love and kisses? I didn't know he had a sense of humour."

"He does not," said Merdyn, filling a flask from a well. "Nor can he read or write. The Vandals pride themselves on their ignorance."

"So who wroteth the letter?" enquired Wolf, who was loading meaty bones into Merdyn's backpack.

"The same person who sent Vanheldon's daughter into the Rivers of Time," Rose answered.

Merdyn smiled and looked at Evanhart. "You see, my love, I told thee she had thy brains."

Evanhart gazed at her descendant proudly.

"But why would a W-blood help Vanheldon?" Merdyn continued. "Vanheldon wanteth revenge. But what does the W-blood wanteth? But, ah . . ." Merdyn shook off these worries and lifted his pack on to his back. "We are wasting time. We must set off now if we are to get to Fort Doom in twelve moons."

"But, Merdyn, thou knowest this is a trap," said a worried Evanhart.

"She's right, Merdyn," Rose added. "They're using

Kris as bait. Like a worm on a hook."

Merdyn looked thoughtful. "I knoweth it is a trap," he said, breaking into a cheeky smile Rose knew so well. "That's why it's lucky I have thee by my side, dear Rose. Vanheldon can't beat the both of us together, can he? Even if he does have help."

Rose loved that Merdyn had faith in her. If only she had faith in herself!

"Thou also have me!" came a voice from a tent behind them. They all looked round to see the young King Arthur barrelling towards them wearing an oversized suit of armour. The poor kid could barely see out of his helmet.

"I shall maketh it my mission to see that no harm cometh to the fair Rose, the princess of Bashingford! After all, I have Excalibur to protecteth us." He raised a very beautiful but heavy-looking sword in the air, the weight of which made him lose his balance and he toppled over and crashed to the ground.

What is with *this guy?* thought Rose. She supposed she ought to be flattered but she just felt embarrassed for him. It was cringey beyond words.

"Nay, nay. Thou must stayeth here, Arthur!" Merdyn insisted. "I would rather thou saw to it that no harm cometh to Evanhart and my children when I am gone."

"Wait!" Evanhart protested suddenly. "Thou meaneth I'm not going with thee?" She already had her backpack on too.

"My darling Evanhart. Light of my life. I understandeth thou wisheth to come. Thou art the bravest person I know. But listen to me, my love . . ." Rose saw how Merdyn looked at Evanhart; he worshipped her. It was how her dad used to look at her mum, like he would have walked to the ends of the earth for her. "If we both go, there is a chance neither of us will come back. And if Lily and Gulliver are to have just one parent, I would want that parent to be thee. A child needeth his mother. Trust me. I knoweth this."

Evanhart was about to protest again until she felt the hands of her children clasping hers. She looked at their pleading eyes and relented. "Then good luck to all of you on your quest," she said. "We will pray for you."

"Rest assured we will returneth, my love," Merdyn reassured her. "Worry thee not. There is no power of darkness on this earth that can defeat the light of love that thou givest me."

And so that night Rose, Merdyn, King Arthur, Wolf and Bubbles set off.

Rose had been touched to see Merdyn hug Evanhart and his children goodbye.

As Evanhart waved them off she pulled her children close.

> *"Ye gods," whispered Evanhart,*
> *"where'er ye are,*
> *Bring them back safe*
> *and be their guiding star."*

CHAPTER THIRTEEN

TWO STRANGERS BOND OVER FOOD FROM A POND

Being held captive in a Dark Ages fort in the middle of what is now Transylvania was not suiting Kris at all. He'd been tied up for two days now. He hadn't been able to even run his hands through his hair, never mind get a comb through it, and as far as getting some expensive product in his luscious locks went? Forget it!

Not that it mattered anyway. There were no fans of Invisiboy here to see him. And even if there were, he'd eaten all the herbs from his belt on the long journey to Romania. He was beginning to think he would never have anyone marvel at his levitation skills again. *This is a very uncool situation*, he thought to himself as he scratched an itch on his lower back against the wooden pole he was tethered to.

"Stop shuffling around!" barked Vanhessa, who

seemed to be his guard. He was being held in the main room off the courtyard. It had a fireplace with some chairs round it and a large slab of stone to one side. The stone had a sort of basin chiselled into it with a plug hole in the bottom. It was such a hodgepodge of a room Kris wondered what you would call it. A kitchen? A lounge-kitchen maybe? A litchen? He scratched his itch again.

"I said, stop shuffling!" ordered Vanhessa again.

"What's the long game plan here?" asked Kris of his captor.

"Merdyn cometh for thee. We killeth Merdyn. End of plan," replied Vanhessa.

Well, she's nothing if not to the point, Kris thought. But there was one glaring omission from her plan list. "And, er . . . what about me?"

"What about thee?" she growled.

"What happens to me after you *killeth* Merdyn?"

Vanhessa looked thoughtful for a second then said, "I knoweth not. Most likely killeth thee too. I do what my father sayeth."

Kris shook his head in pure despair. How could you

reason with these people?
They were savages. Then he remembered
something that his teacher had said after James
Howick had made him put chewing gum in Martha
Richie's hair.

"And if your father told you to jump off a bridge,
would you?"

Vanhessa thought again for a second. "Yes," she said
firmly.

Great, thought Kris. *There's only one way this ends.*

With me dead!

Again, a very uncool situation.

"Can I at least have some food while I wait to die, please? I'm starving!" Kris figured that if he was going to die at the end of this, there was no use playing it nice with these people. "Food please. Now!'

Vanhessa shrugged. She rose to her enormous feet and waddled over to the fireplace. There she ladled a bowl of pottage from the clay pot over the fire, waddled back to Kris and brought it to his lips. Kris guzzled two or three hungry mouthfuls before realising how disgusting it was and spitting it out.

"Bleugh! Oh! Wow! What is that?"

"Pottage." Answered Vanhessa matter-of-factly.

"What's in it?"

"Is food," she grunted. She had a way with words, did Vanhessa.

"Yes, I know that. But what sort of food?"

"Er . . . grains. Beans. Roots. Herbs. Meat. Oh. But we raneth out of meat last week – so is offal."

Kris didn't like the sound of that. It sounded like

someone saying "awful" really quickly.

"What's offal?"

"Offal is animal things like brains, bones, tongue, nose, foot, cheek, knees, eyes."

Kris immediately started retching. I think it was the "eyes" bit that did it.

"Oh my god. Merdyn better hurry up and rescue me because I can't stay here much longer. You're uncivilised."

Vanhessa looked curiously at Kris. "What is un-silly-wised?" she asked.

"Un-civ-il-ised!" Kris emphasised each syllable. "It means you haven't developed yet, you know, as humans. Your hygiene? Your food? Your clothes? Your hair? I mean, it's not surprising, I guess. You've got no mirrors. I guess mirrors haven't been invented yet. You're literally stuck in the Dark Ages."

Vanhessa looked at her clothes and felt her hair,

which had become dirty and a little matted*.

"What be wrong with my hair and clothes?" asked Vanhessa.

Suddenly to Kris she sounded less like a warrior and more like a human being.

"Look. There's nothing wrong per se," he replied gently. "But look at me. Super-white trainers, skinny jeans, stretchy green tee, quilted blue hoodie, Crème de la Bear Hair Fudge. Now look at you. Mud sandals, animal-skin trousers, sheep coat, dead-rat necklace and ACTUAL bear sludge in your hair."

Vanhessa checked that her father and Druilla weren't watching and asked something she'd wanted to ask since she had visited the future.

"The people where thou art from. How do they maketh these shapes with their hair? The clothes? They have such strange colours. What animals be they from?"

---

*The world's first commercial shampoo wouldn't go on sale until 1927. Although the Egyptians used castor and almond oil to protect their hair, the main method of hair care for most people throughout history was "let it do its thing" until around 1600. Having said that, an early hair gel recipe, dating from around 1300, used lizard tallow (animal fat) and swallow droppings. Now that's what you call shampoo. Get it? Swallow droppings? Poo? No? Fine, carry on . . .

Kris broke into a smile. "Girl, you kidnapped the right guy!"

And so the secrets of fashion
Kris did unravel,
Therefore breaking the first
rule of time travel!

CHAPTER FOURTEEN

A MUSE, SOME NEWS
AND
COMPARABLE POOS

Rose, Merdyn and the rescue team had been sailing for over a day and were now only a few hours from mainland Europe. They were on a small wooden boat about the size of two cars. Thankfully, the sea was calm and the weather clement. But on-board tempers were fraying.

Wolf was arguing with Bubbles over who was the better animal.

"A wolf is superior to a guinea pig in every way imaginable. We are faster, more agile, smarter, have sharper teeth . . ."

"Have you *seen* my teeth!" said Bubbles, raging. "They're as sharp as pins!"

"We also have more control over our ablutions," said Wolf.

"Your what?"

"Toilet habits. A canine will go quietly behind a bush and releaseth its faeces, whereas ye guinea pigs appear to drop your hideous brown solids pell-mell*."

"At least our poos are solid and don't stink to high heaven."

"Maybe they don't stinketh to humans, but, remember, wolves' noses are twenty-five times more powerful than humans'**."

"Oooooh," said Bubbles sarcastically, "wolves have twenty-five times more powerful noses than humans! Ooooh! Do you know what you are? You're a snob."

"I knoweth not what that word meaneth but if it meaneth a superior animal then, yes, I am a snob."

"A snob is someone who *thinks* they're better than another animal," replied Bubbles.

"Well, if they *thinketh* it, then they must be—"

"Aaaargh!" Bubbles raged again, then spoke into his Dictaphone. "New rule about dogs: if you EVER meet a

---

*An old word meaning confused or disordered. Its origins are a mystery but it's thought the "mell" part comes from the French verb mesler, which means "to mix". It is a word that can only be used "in action". So if your dad says your messy bedroom is pell-mell, he's using it incorrectly. Correct him by saying, "No, Dad, I just put my clothes away pell-mell!"

**This is true. So next time you think your gran's trumps smell bad, just think about the poor dog!

talking dog, do NOT engage in conversation!"

But let us leave these bickering beasts and join Rose and Arthur elsewhere on the boat.

Since King Arthur had decided he was completely head over heels in love with Rose, it had become a struggle for her to take him seriously. She liked him well enough. He was quite cute. He had blond curly hair with large green eyes and a nose that was slightly upturned so you could always see his nostrils. They flared whenever he got excited, which happened a lot since he'd fallen in love with her. But she just wasn't interested in that sort of thing.

"I have composed a poem for thee, dear Rose," he said after about three minutes of staring into the distance, his tongue sticking out of his mouth in thought. "Would thou like to heareth it?"

"Actually, I might just talk to Merdyn for a bit." Rose began to move but Arthur's next words stopped her.

"Why do thou desire to talketh to Merdyn over me? He is a dull old man. He has no knowledge to impart except 'don't doeth this, don't doeth that'!"

Rose was outraged. "Hey, that's not true! That's

Merlin you're talking about. Where I come from he's famous. And so are you!"

Arthur was very happy to hear this. "Ah, I see. Famous for my good looks and my romantic way with words?"

"No!" said Rose bluntly. "Famous for your bravery and wisdom, which you got from listening to Merdyn."

"Oh, come, come, Rose. Thou soundeth as boring as him now. Here, listen to my poem."

He stood up and cleared his throat.

"Oh Rose! Oh Rose! My love for thee is more bountiful than the freckles upon thy nose . . ."

As King Arthur carried on Rose wondered what Arthur's endgame was? Did he want to marry her? Make her queen? That would be terrible. Well, mostly terrible. Actually, the more she thought about it the more she thought being queen might be all right. She could make up laws – no cruelty to guinea pigs for a start . . . But then she came to her senses. They were on a mission to rescue her brother and get back to the modern world and Arthur was a stuck-up prig who was too much in love with himself to listen to Merdyn/Merlin the Great!

Arthur was still going . . .

"Thy hair is like a cherry tree
in spring—"

"Arthur, please!" she yelled. "No more poems. You can't love me. You don't even know me."

"I do!" protested Arthur.

"All right then. Who's my favourite pop star?"

Arthur went deep into thought before saying triumphantly, "Jupiter!"

"Nope. Beyoncé."

"Bey-on-ceh?" said Arthur, stressing every syllable in the way that people from the Dark Ages do.

"Yes. I rest my case. Now, I'm going to talk to Merdyn. You might not realise it yet, but you need this boring old fool. We all need our elders." Then she went over to Merdyn, who had been steering the ship since they'd set off.

"Goeth easy on the poor fellow," said Merdyn as he saw her approaching. "He's only a pup."

Rose sat down on a little wooden bench next to him. She thought Merdyn was too lenient.

"He's old enough to be king, though, eh? I mean, who puts a twelve-year-old boy in charge of a whole kingdom?

It's ridiculous. The boys at my school can barely tie their shoelaces. He should listen to you. You're cool."

"Ha ha. Thou rememberest me when I was a rascal* . . . "

"I am getting old now, Rose. I am the grandfather of my tribe. I take things a little slower. Young Arthur will learn. He just needeth to find himself. He is lost now, but he will find himself."

Rose could certainly relate to that. "I've been feeling a bit lost lately, Merdyn. I'm happy with my vet clinic but . . . but then Kris got so good at magic and . . ."

Merdyn was excited by this. "Did he now?!"

"Yes! He's much better than me; he's invented all these new spells that I can't do and . . . and . . . I don't know. I think I felt jealous."

"Listen, Rose," said the wise old wizard, "we all have a crisis of confidence from time to time. The trick is to not let it get thee down. To pick thyself back up and keep going. Thou art stronger than thou thinkest, Rose. And *capable* of more than thou thinkest too. Maybe thou were

---

*A mischievous person. Thought to come from the Latin word rasico meaning "to scrape". So if someone calls you a rascal, you can accuse them of scraping the bottom of the barrel with the insult and you won't be wrong!

limiting thyself. Maybe thou needst a little bit of Kris's hufty-tufty instinct?"

"I'm not a hufty-tufty!" Rose protested.

Merdyn chortled again. "And thou never will be, my Rose. But what we W-bloods can do is impressive sometimes. Don't be afraid to impress people. It might even maketh thee a better vet."

"Yeah, well, my vet clinic got destroyed anyway," Rose groaned. "Me and Kris had a fight. It was fair enough. I did destroy his room."

Merdyn laughed heartily. "HA! I bet thy mother was pleased!"

"She banned magic for six months!"

"Ha ha! Good old Suzy." Merdyn remembered her fondly even though they'd never seen eye to eye. "How is she?"

Rose told Merdyn how bad she felt about tricking her mum and travelling back in time without her. "Maybe I should have brought her with me? But I didn't know a non-W-blood could travel through time. Poor Mum. She'll be worried sick by now."

"Your mother is lucky to have a daughter as conscientious as thee. And thou art lucky to have her." There was a thoughtful look in Merdyn's eye, like he was remembering something.

"What were your parents like, Merdyn?" asked Rose. "I've never heard you talk about them before."

"*My* parents? Ha. Well, that's going back a bit," he said, chuckling to himself. 'They were both W-bloods. My father was made court wizard to King Egbert, ooh, fifty years ago now and my mother became very jealous. She thought she should be court wizard; she thoughteth herself the finest W-blood in all the land, much better than my father."

"And *was* she better than your father?"

"Oh yes. Very much so. But there had never been a court witch before. It was unheard of and King Egbert, well, let's just say he was not a person that liketh to break with tradition. Still, my mother was strong-willed and couldn't get over being snubbed by the king. She was so angry she decided to leaveth the family home for a land where she was more appreciated. Before she left she madeth me choose between them. Stayeth with my father or goeth with her. It was the most terrible moment of my life. Every child's worst nightmare. But . . . I couldn't leaveth my home. I had friends here. I had the school of alchemy. I had Evanhart. So I choseth to stay with my father."

Rose listened intently. "And what happened to your mother? Where did she go?"

"I knoweth not. She said she was going to proveth herself the best W-blood in the world."

"And did she succeed?"

"No. Sadly not. I heard she died attempting a flying spell off a hundred-metre cliff. That was my mother. Nobody else was good enough but she . . . she was capable of anything. That's why thou should feel lucky that thy mother worries about thee. To worry about someone means thou love them. And there's nothing wrong with that."

Rose marvelled at how wise her old friend had become. How different he was to the man she had met when he visited the modern world. She liked it. And that fool King Arthur should like it too.

> *Now there could be no debate*
> *Why they called him*
> *Merdyn the Great.*

CHAPTER FIFTEEN

KNOW-IT-ALLS
AND
CRYSTAL BALLS

Kris knew everything there was to know about fashion and he'd thoroughly enjoyed giving Vanhessa a complete rundown of trends and fads in hair and clothes throughout the ages. He had just got up to the 1980s . . .

"And they achieved the big-hair look by using crimping irons."

"Crimping irons . . .?" repeated Vanhessa with a large smile.

Suddenly the door from the courtyard opened and Druilla entered, carrying her crystal ball. "I have good news for thee, Kris."

"Have my crimping irons arrived?"

Kris aimed his joke at Vanhessa, who had to stifle a laugh in front of the evil witch.

"Merdyn has launched a rescue party," the old lady

said, ignoring Kris's quip. "They have boarded a ship and saileth the Frisian Sea* as we speak."

"Righto," said Kris. Unlike Rose, Kris was never short of self-confidence, even when he was tethered to a stake in place called Fort Doom. "And, er . . . where are you getting this intel?"

"Why, my crystal ball," Druilla replied to the cheeky boy.

"Ah, yes. I've been meaning to talk to you about that actually."

"About what?"

"About the crystal ball."

"What about it?"

"Well, it's just a bit clichéd, isn't it?"

"What do thou mean, clichéd?" enquired Druilla. She was now getting irritated, but Kris was rather enjoying himself. He wasn't scared of this old lady. Now Vanheldon, with his bearskins and enormous, barrel-like chest, HE was scary. This old lady with a walking stick? No, no.

"I mean, they're ten a penny where I come from.

---

*The North Sea was known as the Frisian Sea from Roman times until quite recently. Frisia was the bits of Germany and the Netherlands that border the coast.

Every quack in town has a crystal ball. We had a fortune teller at the school fair once; she had a crystal ball too."

Druilla snapped at the insolent boy, "I'll have thee know I *invented* the crystal ball! I cleft it with my own bloodied hands from the Carpathian Mountains themselves!"

"Oh yeah? Our school fortune teller got hers from eBay."

Vanhessa had been listening to all this with glee – she didn't much like Druilla either – and she let out a little giggle.

Druilla looked momentarily bewildered, like a grandma who had lost control of her grandchildren. But suddenly a man's voice cut through the giggles.

"WHAT IS THE MEANING OF THIS MIRTH?" It was Vanheldon. He heaved his giant frame through the door and slapped his daughter in the face. The noise was like an enormous wet fish slapping against a garage door.

SHLAPPAPAP!!

Then he turned to Kris and gave him TWO slaps.

SHLAP-SHAPPAPAP!!

"Daughter? Remember this boy is a prisoner. He is not to be engaged with. Do so again and you shall feel my wrath a thousand-fold."

"Yes, Father," Vanhessa mumbled and stood to attention.

Kris's ears were still ringing like church bells.

"Did thou show the boy the happy news?" the vast Vandal asked Druilla.

"I was just about to when he began mocking me. Here . . ." she said, offering up the crystal ball to Kris, before adding sarcastically, "look into my *'clichéd'* crystal ball."

Kris looked into the ball and saw images of people. It was like watching an old TV set from the 1950s he'd seen in a museum; the images were frayed round the edges but as real as anything. He saw the unmistakeable shape of Merdyn board the ship followed by a wolf, a boy of twelve barely able to carry his sword and then, who was this? A girl? But a girl wearing jeans and a jacket with an animal poking out of the pocket? Was that?

A guinea pig? But . . .

Now here the reader might wonder how Kris didn't recognise Rose immediately. But, remember, for all he knew they were still at war. The last time they spoke his sister had said she wished she'd never had a brother and he'd said he wished he had a different sister. And now here she was – yes, it was DEFINITELY Rose! – on a mission to rescue him. Walking straight into a trap! For reasons he couldn't quite fathom yet poor Kris burst out crying.

"Yeeees!" crowed Druilla. "'Tis your sister Rose. She must truly loveth thee to traverse the Rivers of Time in a bid to save thy wretched life. Not laughing at me now, art thou?!"

"Please!!" Kris blubbed. "Don't hurt her. Please!"

"Oh, we have no intention of HURTING HER," boomed Vanheldon, enjoying himself now. "We intendeth to KILL her!" And he laughed so hard the whole fort shook. "HA HA HA! We're going to KILL ALL OF THEM!!"

Vanheldon and Druilla both looked gleefully back into the crystal ball.

Kris's face streamed with tears as he thought about his dear little sister.

She had come all this way
to rescue him,
And now both their futures
looked very grim.

CHAPTER SIXTEEN

ENCHANTED WATER FLOWS AND A FOUL WIND BLOWS

Young King Arthur had just completed his seventeenth "Ode to Rose" of their journey across the sea when the first winds blew. Rose never thought she'd feel relieved to witness a life-threatening weather system move in, but at least it made Arthur think of something else for a change.

"I do not liketh this, sire," said Wolf. "My canine instincts telleth me we're in trouble," he added, rather haughtily Bubbles thought.

"Oh, your canine instincts, eh?" the guinea pig said with a dollop of sarcasm. "Wanna know what tells me we're in trouble? *My eyes!* It's obvious, mate. There's an actual, literal hurricane coming!"

Rose didn't know what was going on between the two pets but she didn't like what her eyes were seeing either. She could just about make out the shore of mainland Europe;

it was so close, but there were rolling thunderclouds heading towards them, dark and foreboding, like soot billowing from an enormous fireplace.

Then they felt a wind. WHOOOOSH! But it was no ordinary wind. It seemed to have no sense of direction. It first blew from the east. Then the west. Then seemed to swirl around in circles with great ferocity. It was like someone had given a toddler the most powerful hairdryer in the world and they were just having fun with it.

Merdyn tried to bring the sail in but the wind suddenly gusted and tore it from its mast. It unfurled and went flapping over the waves like a crisp packet over a puddle (blown by a hairdryer held by a playful toddler).

"Hold fast!" shouted Merdyn. "Hold on to anything ye can!"

Arthur instinctively grabbed Rose.

"Not me, you idiot!" she hollered. "The flipping boat!" And she pushed him down to the deck of the ship and made him grip one of the struts while she clung to the mast.

Merdyn saw the first big wave coming and steered the front of the ship into it.

CROOSH! The boat crashed through the wave and took off into the air before slapping down on to the surface of the sea like one of Vanheldon's face slaps. **SHLAP!**

"Everybody all right?!" shouted Merdyn as the wind howled around them and water flew this way and that.

Very wet yelps of "yes/fine/worry not, sire/sort of" came from the direction of Rose, Arthur, Wolf and Bubbles.

"We can rideth this out! Hold tight and we'll be fine!" Merdyn yelled.

But in his heart Merdyn knew they were NOT going to be fine as he spotted even darker clouds and even bigger waves coming towards them.

"Gadsbudlikins*!" he muttered to himself. "What unnatural doings have caused this?"

---

*The literal translation is "God's little body". Try saying this instead of OMG. It's much more original!

The answer lay many miles away in darkest Transylvania. Kris had wondered what Druilla was doing when she had filled the stone sink in the lounge/kitchen with water. She uttered a foul-sounding incantation, the like of which he'd never heard before.

"LEADEROX, LICHENFESTEN, AGUAMIRICALIS!!"

She then got a small piece of wood no bigger than a matchbox, and wedged a stick in one of its grooves. She tore a square of cloth from her filthy dress and skewered it through the stick, so it made a small sail. It was a boat, Kris realised, a tiny toy boat. She put it on the water and recited another incantation.

"LEECHIFEX, BLOWTIS, HURRICANUS!!"

Then she cackled with glee as she blew the sails this way and that and swirled her finger in the water. She kept glancing back at her crystal ball. Kris couldn't see what was being shown in the ball until Vanhessa moved it slightly when Druilla wasn't looking.

Then he wished he hadn't! For there was Rose clinging

to a sailing ship that was being blasted by winds and blown this way and that. DRUILLA that was causing the storm! She was performing some of the darkest magic imaginable in that stone sink, remotely manipulating the air with her breath and the water with her fingers. It was a magic so powerful Kris could barely believe his eyes.

"Killeth Merdyn now, Druilla!" thundered the very excited Vanheldon.

"Patience, Vanheldon. The games are just beginning." And then Druilla delved into her pocket and took out a jar containing two rather evil-looking lizards. "Wait till they meeteth my fire salamanders*!"

Druilla gleefully popped open the lid of the jar and let the two nasty-looking creatures slide out into the murky water of the stone sink. They were each twice the size of the toy boat, and Kris knew what this meant. Rose and Merdyn would soon have company in the shape of two giant reptiles.

"NO!" shouted Kris. "Please stop!"

"QUIET!" snapped Vanheldon. Kris fell silent,

----
*Large newt-like creatures that live in the woodlands of Eastern Europe. Fire salamanders are black with yellow stripes, and can still be found today, though their numbers are declining.

fearing another slap to end all slaps. "If thou screamest like that, we won't be able to heareth *their* screams. Isn't that right, Druilla?"

She and Vanheldon laughed as they watched the fire salamanders circle the boat.

"Vanhessa, come. Watch!" Vanheldon said.

Vanhessa walked slowly over to the sink, but in truth she felt for Kris, who was trying once more to wriggle out of the ropes tying him to the wooden pole. Vanhessa had watched her beloved sister, Vinhella, die on the battlefield defeated by the Celts. It was not easy feeling powerless while your sister was in danger.

Her disgust for Druilla
she was concealing.
Poor Kris.
She knew how he was feeling.

CHAPTER SEVENTEEN

OF LARGE LIZARDS AND POWERFUL WIZARDS

After being tossed about on the waves like a toy boat, Merdyn and the others felt the ship steady as the storm suddenly disappeared. The waves were gone, the black clouds were replaced by glorious sunshine, the wind stilled to barely a breath. Once again they could see the shoreline in the distance. Rose took a deep breath. They were home and dry now, surely?

From Rose's jacket pocket, where Bubbles had kept his head firmly down, could be heard the click of a Dictaphone and a little voice. "List of terrible modes of transport: number one, boats; number two, boats; number three, boats . . ."

Arthur laughed, standing upright and doing his best to wave his sword in the air. "That's because I threatened to useth Excalibur upon thee, isn't it? Take that,

Mother Nature!"

"Quiet, Arthur," spoke Merdyn. "I fear this be not the work of Mother Nature."

Rose also sensed the danger might not be over. "What is it, Merdyn?"

"Dark magic," Wolf replied for the great wizard.

"Aye," said Merdyn. "I senseth dark magic like I never have before."

"What's dark magic?" asked Rose.

"Most magic, even that used by warlocks, deriveth from light, from nature. But dark magic useth the forces of meanness, of evil. It is a power that lurketh in us all, but it must not be used for it feedeth on the soul of a person and leaveth them hollow like a dead tree trunk."

"Erm, I don't want to be the bearer of bad news –" Bubbles had stopped making his list and had instead become concerned by the vibrations he'd been feeling in his tiny feet – "but I think there's something big swimming under the boat. And when I say something big, I literally, actually mean something BIG and I'm not joking."

Everybody looked over the side of the boat but saw

nothing but calm, still water.

"Are you sure, Bubbles?" asked Rose.

"Yes!" squeaked the guinea pig. "I feel it in my tootsies! A guinea pig's tootsies never lie!"

"He's making it up," barked the snooty Wolf.

"I am not making it up. I'll have you know that due to my small size I'm able to sense vibrations that more bulbous animals can't!"

"Art thou calling me bulbous?" Wolf growled and the two started squabbling again.

"Shhhhhh!" Rose had spotted something, something smooth and black breaking the surface of the water. "There! Look!" Everybody could now see the dark slimy skin of an enormous sea creature. And there wasn't just one; there were two.

"I liketh not the look of these beasts," said Merdyn.

"What are they?" wondered Arthur.

Rose looked closely at the creatures. Each time they broke the surface they revealed more of themselves. The black skin was striped with yellow flashes, like the flames of a fire. "They aren't sea creatures at all," she said in a grave tone.

"Hello?" quipped Bubbles, eager to point out the obvious. "They are both *creatures*, and they're *in the sea*."

"I'm telling you they don't belong in the sea. They're fire salamanders."

Bubbles didn't like the sound of them. "I think I preferred sea creatures,' he said with a tremble in his voice.

If the oversized beasts were spoiling for a fight – and they were circling the boat, he noticed – Merdyn wanted to know more about them. "Tell us about these fire salamanders, Rose."

"We had one brought into my clinic, so I did some research. They're carnivores. They eat spiders, worms and even newts and young frogs. They tend to stalk their prey with their eyes above water—"

Right on cue, the salamanders raised their huge black eyes out of the water.

"Then what do they do?" asked Arthur, suddenly interested.

"Then they quietly dive back under the water . . ."

Again, the salamanders did exactly what Rose was

describing, silently sinking beneath the surface of the sea.

"*And then?*" Wolf asked, the haughtiness in his voice replaced by abject terror.

"Then they attack their prey from beneath."

There was a beat of silence after Rose had spoken these words – then Merdyn screamed

"HOLD ON!"

and they all grabbed the mast. But it was too late.

THUMP!

The first salamander almost lifted the boat clean out of the water but it stayed intact.

THUMP!

The second salamander struck the boat but our intrepid rescue team weren't so lucky this time and the boat broke apart, sending them all into the water.

Meanwhile, in Vanheldon's fort, Druilla chirped with delight as she watched the salamanders circling the broken little boat. "Now why don't ye have your lunch, my pretties. Eat those INSECTS!"

Kris was desperate. But he could see that Vanhessa was distressed about what Druilla was doing. Vanheldon was bent over the sink, laughing heartily, but Vanhessa was standing near Kris with her eyes closed and her fists clenched.

"Psssst! Vanhessa," he whispered. "Please untie my hand. Just one. It'll look like I wriggled free. I can't let them kill my little sister! Please, Vanhessa. Look into your heart."

Vanhessa opened her eyes and saw tears running down the side of Kris's face. She looked into Druilla's crystal ball and saw Rose bobbing helplessly up and down in the water. She couldn't possibly help Kris, could she? If her father noticed, there was no knowing what he would do, but she didn't want Kris to watch his sister being eaten alive!

Back in the sea, Rose, Merdyn, Arthur, Wolf and Bubbles were treading water. Arthur clung to a piece of the broken boat and held out a hand to Rose. They watche in horror as the circling salamanders, each as big as a single-decker bus, dived down to make another attack. Bubbles whimpered.

"Everybody spread out!" Rose hollered. "If we stay in a pack, they'll come up underneath and eat us all in one go!"

Everybody swam away from each other. Merdyn and Bubbles were strong swimmers. Rose used her perfect breaststroke, while Arthur was more doggy-paddle, as was Wolf for obvious reasons.

"Rose!" cried Merdyn. "Thou art the animal expert. Do thou have a spell? Something that could control them?"

Rose wracked her brains then realised that, yes . . . yes, she did! She had an animal-taming spell she used on wild animals to calm them down but she'd never used it on anything this big.

She realised she'd better remember it sharpish as

a salamander WHOOSHED up from underneath Merdyn, its mouth wide open. Then: RAAAAA! The other salamander leaped out of the water, taking Arthur in its mouth.

As the salamander bit down on Arthur, it got its teeth stuck on the plank of wood that Arthur was using as a float. The salamander bit down on the plank of wood with all its might but it only cracked. Rose could see Arthur trying to draw his sword.

Meanwhile, Merdyn had used his trusty staff to wedge open his salamander's mouth, but neither he nor Arthur had much time before these would break and they became amphibian food.

"How's that spell coming along, Rose?" boomed Merdyn from inside the creature's straining mouth.

Rose was flustered. "Erm . . .

ANIMA BUFFONEM KEEPICALMICUS!"

She screamed but nothing happened. "No. Wait. Not 'BUFFONEM', 'CRUFONEM'. No. erm . . ."

"Anytime soon, Rose!" roared Arthur. The plank of

wood that was holding his salamander's mouth open was snapping as the creature's jaw crushed it.

Rose tried again. "I've got it now.

ANIMA TRUFONEM KEEPICALMICUS!"

But again nothing happened. Rose needed to throw lavender on the creatures or the spell wouldn't work. She reached down to her herb pouches on her belt, now underwater, but they were empty. The herbs must have spilled out into the water!

"I've no lavender! I can't do it!" she cried. "I'm so sorry!"

"It's all right. I heardeth thy spell. I can do it." Merdyn closed his eyes for a second as if to summon some inner power and his staff started to glow as if it were lit up by a bulb inside.

"ANIMA TRUFONEM KEEPICALMICUS!"

Merdyn chanted. All of a sudden his salamander stopped thrashing around and became docile. Standing in the open mouth of the tamed animal, Merdyn repeated the spell on Arthur's salamander. He'd barely finished when the piece of wood that had been wedging the great beast's mouth open snapped and Arthur jumped out just in time. The creature became quiet and still.

"I'm sorry, Merdyn," said Rose, still upset that she hadn't completed her spell.

Merdyn smiled at her. "It's all right, Rose. We did it together. It was good teamwork."

This made Rose feel a little better – but not much. What if that had happened when Merdyn wasn't around to help her? Everyone would have been eaten alive.

"Now then,' said Merdyn, turning to the giant salamanders, "as ye very rudely smashethed our boat, how about giving us a ride to land?"

A few moments later, Rose experienced something she never thought would happen in her wildest dreams. She was riding to shore on the back of a giant salamander. She was clinging on to Merdyn and Merdyn was clinging on to a slimy tuft of skin on the salamander's neck, steering it if it went off track. Merdyn was clearly loving every second.

"WHEEEEEEEEEEEEEEEE!" he cried from time to time.

Even Bubbles was having fun. From inside Rose's pocket he pressed record on his Dictaphone. "Recommendation for holidaymakers of all ages: salamander surfing! It's fun, it's safe, it's eco-friendly. Literally."

"Driving" the other salamander was young King Arthur, who was beginning to see Merdyn in a new light. Maybe Rose was right, maybe he wasn't so dull. "WHEEEEEEEEEEEEEEEEEEEEE!" he cried too.

Clinging on to Arthur's trousers with his teeth was Wolf. "I knew it would all be right in the end," he muttered, his haughtiness coming back. "Call it canine intuition."

But back in Vanheldon's fort somebody wasn't so happy.

Vanheldon spoke first. "Merdyn gotteth away!"

Druilla smirked. "They thinketh they have, but now I shall sendeth a wave to killeth them all!" she said and cackled.

As Druilla prepared her wave spell, Kris spotted some dill leaves lying on a shelf. *The herb they use in the pottage is dill?* he thought to himself. If only he could free his hand! He made one last plea to Vanhessa.

"Please, Vanhessa. See that herb over there, the dill? I need it. And I need you to free my hand. I have to stop Druilla killing my sister!"

"Quiet!" Vanhessa whisper-shouted.

"Vanhessa, please! Rose and I had a fight last time we spoke. I *need* to see her again. I *need* to say sorry!"

Vanhessa had had the same thing with her sister. They had fallen out over a Goth boy before Vanhella was killed and she'd never had the chance to say sorry. The Goth boy wasn't even that strong!

Druilla was just finishing her wave spell –

"FRATALIN WAVICUS TSUNAMICA!"

when she heard another spell . . .

"HOLCUS CRACKAJACKA!"

. . . and was hit by lightning coming from Kris's direction.

"W-what the—?" she stammered, reeling backwards, before seeing Kris had freed one hand.

"Lightning Boy to the rescue!" Kris shouted, perhaps needlessly, I must admit, before hurling more dill leaves and sending another lightning bolt at the stone sink.

"HOLCUS CRACKAJACKA!"

This bolt cracked the sink and the water spilled out and drained away. The two salamanders scampered away.

"My water! My precious magic water!" Druilla screamed. "Damn thee, boy!"

Druilla marched up to Kris, who was feeling very pleased with himself. But his luck was about to change.

"So, thou art a W-blood too, eh?" said Druilla. "Thou kepteth that quiet, didn't thou?"

"Not really," said Kris, again opening his mouth when

he really should have kept it closed, if you ask me. "It's just I had my hands tied behind my back so—"

Before he could finish his sentence Druilla had raised her fingers to his forehead.

"Ow!" cried Kris, feeling an intense pain in his head. "What are you doing?!"

"I'm stealing thy magic from thee." Druilla spoke so calmly Kris thought he'd misheard her, but when he saw particles of light emanating from his forehead and making their way to Druilla's fingers he knew she was serious. How could he stop her? He thought and thought. But all his invisibility and levitating spells wouldn't save him now.

As Druilla sucked the magic from him, she became years younger. The wrinkles around her eyes receded and the skin round her neck firmed up and her grey hair turned a shade of black. By the time she had drained ALL Kris's magic she was almost, well, beautiful.

She withdrew her fingers from his forehead and looked at the new youthful skin on her hands. "More light," she said softly to herself. "More light to turneth into darkness."

Then she turned on the gawping Vandals. "Thee!"

she snapped at Vanheldon. "Fixeth that sink stone."

Vanheldon paused for a second. *Who's in charge here?* he thought, but he couldn't risk upsetting the mad witch lest she sucked his brains out too. He nodded vigorously.

"And thee!" Druilla turned to Vanessa now. "Tiest him up properly this time. Not that there is much he can do now he has no powers. Eh, *Lightning boy*?!" She cackled and then marched out of the room.

Kris felt empty and exhausted, like he'd had all the life hoovered out of his soul. He hadn't felt this exhausted since the PE teacher Mr Bradshaw had made him do a half marathon even though he had a stomach bug!

Vanessa tied Kris up again. "I'm sorry," she whispered in his ear as she did so.

"Don't be sorry," Kris replied weakly, his lips almost too dry to talk.

"But she tooketh thy magic," Vanessa said in a hushed voice, being careful that her father didn't hear her as he started to fix the sink stone.

"At least I saved my sister," Kris whispered back.

All the times that Rose had said he needed to do good

with his magic – now he knew why. He was crushed that his powers were gone. Devastated. He wept for Fantastikid. Magiboy was no more! But he had to admit, saving Rose and Merdyn's life felt a sight better than stealing some expensive hair cream! He finally understood what Rose had been telling him all along.

It was as loud and clear now
as a jumbo jet.
But did he wish he'd learned
his lesson sooner? You bet!

CHAPTER EIGHTEEN

OF SUPERFISHES AND TASTY DISHES

The giant salamanders deposited Rose and the rescue party on the shore before slipping back into the sea and disappearing as if they had been sucked down a plughole. (Funny that, eh?)

The waves lapped the sandy beach and the sun shone brightly.

"Let us stay awhile and frolic in the waters!" Arthur insisted, but Merdyn held up a hand.

"There is no time to frolic, Arthur. We are here to save Kris, remember? Thou must learneth that when an important task is at hand thou must putteth thy mind to it and nothing else. Come. Though we are weary we must walketh."

Fun Merdyn is no more, thought Arthur as they all began to trudge off. *What was he famous for in Rose's time?*

Being the most boring man ever?

As they walked, Rose gathered the herbs and grasses she needed to replenish her herb belt. She marvelled at the abundance of plants here in the Dark Ages. At home she would have to cycle to the local organic shop, but here she barely needed to stray from the path. There was rosemary, thyme, dill, parsley, dandelion, lavender, hog root and milk thistle all within grasping distance. It was a witch's heaven. But Rose still felt a little inadequate. How had Merdyn conjured magic without herbs? She was about to jog on and ask him when Arthur bowled up with a question of his own.

"Rose, I senseth that my love for thee is not being returned."

"Your senses are correct," said Rose matter-of-factly. "But it's no biggie. Just be cool about it."

"'Cool'? Thou wanteth me to lower my temperature? I do not thinketh this is possible."

Rose quickly realised the word "cool" had changed a lot over the years. "No, no. 'Cool' in my time also means to take it easy. Or you say it when something is impressive.

Like, 'that was cool'."

"So thou art saying I'm NOT 'cool'?!" Arthur's eyes filled with fake tears. "How can thou crush my heart like 'twere but a bug beneath thy feet?! Any woman should jump at the chance to marry a king."

"OK. Look." Rose sighed. "You seem very nice, but, firstly, I'm not a woman, I'm twelve. And anyway, where I'm from women don't get married till their twenties or thirties if at all."

"If at all?!" Arthur could hardly believe his ears. "What?!! That is most peculiar."

"And secondly I don't know what you love about me. Is it my hair? My glasses?"

"Yes, and also thy freckles and thy lovely nose."

"Right. That's what I mean. Those are superficial things."

"Superfish things? What is 'superfish'? Ah. Thou mean a big fish? Where?"

"No. *Superficial*. It means shallow. Surface things. Now, if you said you loved my brain, that would be different."

King Arthur guffawed loudly. "Thy brain? Ha. I could never love a brain. I saw one once. In a dead rabbit. They are hideous grey slimy knobbly things. No one in their right mind could possibly love one."

Rose could tell it was going to be hard getting through to this boy. "All right, let me put it another way. Girls aren't just for marrying. We could be friends, for example. How about that?"

Arthur was going to laugh again but paused for thought this time. "Huh. Friends with a girl?" he mused. "It's . . . *possible*, I suppose."

Rose felt she was getting through so she pushed on. "And, look, you're young. You probably haven't figured out what you're all about."

"Oh, I have," replied Arthur firmly. "I pulled the sword from the stone, didn't I? I'm king. Now I just need to findeth a queen and liveth happily ever after."

"Well then, my advice to you would be to find something else to focus on," said Rose. "You're king. You have great power. And with great power comes great responsibility."

Arthur gasped in awe. "Rose, thou art so wise."

"Actually, that's a line from *Spider-man*," Rose confessed.

"*Spider-man?*" Arthur repeated, intrigued. "Tell me, who is this . . . Spider-man?"

Rose realised the mistake she'd made. "Oh no, forget I said that. That's a can of worms I should never really have opened."

Now Arthur was even more intrigued. "Thou eat *cans of worms* where thou art from?"

Sighing, Rose did her best to explain what she was talking about without giving too much information about the future – which was difficult – but at least they were having a proper conversation at last!

When night came, they stopped somewhere in the modern-day Netherlands. They set up camp near one of many rivers that ran through the land and lit a fire. Arthur had gone to find more firewood and Merdyn was cooking some pottage in a little pot.

It was quite chilly and Bubbles was annoyed that Wolf was lying right next to the fire, stopping the heat from getting to him.

"Why do you have to lie so close? You're, like, almost literally *in* the fire!" he complained, shivering dramatically.

"Canines are warm-blooded animals. We need fire to heateth our bodies on cold nights."

"*I'm* a warm-blooded animal too!" claimed Bubbles with confidence, then he turned to Rose. "Aren't I?"

"Yes," said Rose. "But Wolf is bigger than you so he will require more heat to warm him up, that's why he sits so close."

Bubbles could scarcely believe his ears. "Whose side are you on?!"

"Besides, I have sea water in my ears and nose. I'm trying to dryeth them out," Wolf grumbled, waggling his head from side to side to prove his discomfort.

"Aha!" said Bubbles. "Guinea pigs don't have that problem. We can close our ear canals and nasal cavities to stop water getting in. This is from when we used to be aquatic animals. Isn't that right, Rose?"

"Yes, Bubbles, but no one likes a hufty tufty," she reminded him.

"Ha! Yes, be quiet, thou hufty tufty," said Wolf, smirking.

"Hey, she can call me a hufty tufty – you can't!"

Rose decided to leave the bickering animals and went to sit near Merdyn.

"How did you do that back there?" she asked him as the flames flickered dappled light upon their faces. "How did you do my spell without any herbs? Spells come from nature, right?"

Merdyn grinned his mischievous grin. "Correct. And where does nature cometh from but from light?"

"Light?" said Rose, confused.

Merdyn stopped stirring the pottage pot and explained. "Light maketh the plants grow; it feedeth all of nature. Without it nature withers and dies. I have been trying lately to harness the power of light for my magic. It taketh concentration and great stillness of the mind. Thou must *feel* the human connection to nature. I mean, *really* feel it. 'Tis difficult. But by the heavens is it worth it."

Merdyn's smile faded as he seemed to remember something. He tried to cover it up. "Here, fetch a bowl. This stew is ready."

"Merdyn, what is it?" asked Rose, concerned.

Merdyn took a deep breath. "When I was in thy world I was heading towards a path of darkness but thou taughtest me to use my power for good. Thou showed me the light. Since then I have been working on the power of light and it has been fruitful. But what happeneth today? That dark magic? It was so powerful. Whoever is doing it wanteth to bring darkness to the whole world. I fear there is a great battle ahead. A battle betwixt good and evil."

"But good will win, right?" said Rose. "I mean, the history books say the Dark Ages end and the age of Enlightenment begins?"

"Rose, don't thou understandeth? Thou art in the past now. The history books have yet to be written. If we loseth against the forces of darkness, goodness knows what will be waiting for thee when thou getteth back to the future. If thou ever getteth back at all . . ."

Rose felt a sense of panic in these strange lands. The future of the world was in their hands.

CHAPTER NINETEEN

TWO FRIENDS TALK ALL DAY AND TWO STRANGERS ENTER THE FRAY

After Vanhessa had risked so much to help Kris, they began to have frequent chats about the differences between the modern world and the Dark Ages. Over the next few days they discussed food, transport, hairstyles, buildings, and learned a great deal from each other. Vanhessa picked up things pretty quickly and she soon tried to copy Kris's jokes. For example, he enjoyed adding "not" at the end of an affirmative statement, like, "You know I really like being held prisoner in this fort. NOT!" Vanhessa found this amusing so used it herself from time to time. For example, "I like picking flowers and smelling them. NOT!"

One day they were laughing and joking while Vanheldon and Druilla were busy at the other side of the room.

"You know, Vanhessa," remarked Kris after another brilliant "NOT!" line from the young warrior, "if you weren't a baddie, I think we could have been friends."

Vanhessa looked confused. "What do thou meaneth? A *baddie*."

"You know, the villains."

"*Villains?*"

"Yeah. You know how I told you we have these things called movies about heroes, like Superman and Batman?"

Vanhessa smiled at the memory. "Ah yes. I liketh the sound of this *bat man*."

"Well, they do *kind* things like save a cat who's got stuck in a tree or something. But the baddies, they do evil things like. er . . . I dunno, like killing people for fun."

Vanhessa became very upset. "Oh no. We do not killeth people for fun. No, no, never *fun*."

"Right, well, no offence, but you were going to kill me, remember? When you found out I wasn't Rose? And I presume you're going to kill me once you've killed Merdyn, or your dad will. I'm just guessing here. Am I right?"

"Oh yes, of course," Vanhessa admitted, a little caught

out, "but it won't be fun . . . I don't think."

Truth was, she didn't know what to think any more. Kris was asking questions she'd never even thought about for a second. "Kris, telleth me more about these . . . baddies?" she said.

On the other side of the room, Vanheldon was just finishing plugging up the sink stone after fixing it. Druilla was sketching a map with chalk on a piece of slate*.

"There. It is all done. One sink. Fixed," announced Vanheldon proudly.

Druilla ignored him and carried on doodling. Vanheldon was still a little alarmed about the change in status between them. Now she was looking less like an old hag and more like an evil sorceress with powers a billion times stronger than him, he was getting a little insecure to say the least.

"Erm, Druilla?" he started tentatively. "What be the plan here? We both have the same goal. To destroy Merdyn. I am ready. With sword in hand, warrior cry at the ready. Yet thou drawest on slate in silence. I am not

---

*The earliest evidence of pen and paper use was in Spain in 1150. Imagine a whole classroom filled with kids writing with chalk on slate. Scratch, scritch, squeak!

complaining. It's just I think we ought to killeth Merdyn sooner rather than later."

"Oh dear," groaned Druilla. "Ye Vandals! Always ready with your swords. Patience, my animal-skin-loving friend. Do not worry thyself about Merdyn. I have the situation under control. I would be more worried about thy daughter."

Druilla dropped this bombshell without once looking up. It took Vanheldon completely by surprise.

"What about my daughter?" he asked.

Druilla gestured towards the wooden stake on the other side of the room where Kris was tied up.

Vanhessa was getting some fashion tips from him. She was accessorising her smock with a belt here, a rolled-up sleeve there. All the while, they were making each other giggle like teenagers, which is what they were after all.

"She does no wrong." Vanheldon said, his fatherly instinct kicking in. "She is merely keeping up the spirits of the prisoner. After all, he is no use to us melancholic or dead."

Druilla pondered. "Hmm . . . maybe. But I thinketh

she is beginning to have . . . *sympathies* with the prisoner."

"Nonsense!" protested Vanheldon. "She is a little sensitive sometimes. Like her mother. But she is a warrior through and through. And committed to my – to *our* – cause."

"If thou sayest so," said Druilla wearily.

"I do sayeth so!" replied Vanheldon forcefully, but he glanced anxiously again at his daughter, who was now feeding Kris some pottage with a spoon.

"One more thing," Druilla added ominously as she picked up her crystal ball.

"What is it?" Vanheldon asked nervously. He didn't like her tone of voice.

"Someone else cometh," Druilla announced calmly.

Vanheldon was confused. "What do thou meaneth 'someone else'?"

"Exactly what I said. Someone else. I see *two* more people in the ball. A day or so behind Merdyn and his gang of fools. Do thou recognise them?"

She thrust her crystal ball for him to look at, but all he could make out were two human-looking shadows walking side by side. The shadows were blurred around the edges, like someone had put a layer of grease over them.

"What am I looking at? I cannot see their faces."

"Neither can I. Which means one or both of them must be a W-blood. They are using a clouding spell. Which means they knoweth that they might be being watched. Which means they are very clever. Which makes me wonder why I'm showing it to thee, as if thou would know any clever people!" And with that she turned her back on him and walked out of the room.

She can be very rude, Vanheldon thought to himself. Then he realised he had not been mistaken. She really did think she was in charge now. And, what was worse, he was beginning to think so too.

But did he think
there would not be a hitch
If he sought the help
of a powerful witch?!

CHAPTER TWENTY

WILD HORSES
AND
MAGICAL FORCES

Kris's rescue team marched day and night. They walked in single file. Wolf, being the fastest, would go ahead and make sure there were no nasty surprises such as bears, bandits and even the odd tiger*.

Behind Wolf was Merdyn, then Arthur, who wanted to be in front of Rose to protect her with his life. Bubbles insisted on sitting in Rose's backpack, facing backwards. Not to be outdone by Wolf, Bubbles claimed to be "bringing up the rear". This seemed to Rose to consist of him shouting "All clear at the back!" every ten minutes, and making overly dramatic recordings in his diary like "Day three, the sun blazes down like a big hot lemon." The whole effect of his behaviour on Rose after four days was exhausting.

----

*Caspian tigers were known to travel into northern Europe, hence the tigers' teeth on the Vandals' necklaces. (The Vandals weren't big on conservation.) Sadly these tigers are now extinct. (I wonder why?!)

Merdyn knew he couldn't risk his group travelling by water or by air in case the dark magic of whoever was helping Vanheldon reached them again. He explained to Rose that dark magic needs fluidity. It can be carried on the air or via water but not through the earth, so they would have to travel on land. But that didn't mean they couldn't speed the journey up a little bit. They needed to go faster if they were to surprise the enemy. And for this Merdyn had a cunning plan.

One moonlit night, when they had almost reached Bohemia (modern-day Czech Republic), Merdyn called for the gang to stop and be quiet.

"Shhhhh. They're here," he whispered.

"Who's here?" Rose asked.

Merdyn ushered the gang past the last of the trees in the forest they'd been walking in, to a scene that took Rose's breath away. It was an enormous grassy plain that stretched as far as the eye could see. And on that plain, dotted here and there, were hundreds of wild horses.

"They are tarpans**, to use their proper name,"

** The tarpan or Eurasian wild horse (Equus ferus ferus) was once very common in northern Europe but was hunted to extinction by the end of the nineteenth century. The last known tarpan died in captivity in Russia in 1909.

Merdyn informed the others. "I hoped they would be here."

Rose gasped, as they tiptoed quietly between the huge beasts. "Wow! They're beautiful." They were almost pure white with black spots. *Like Dalmatians*, Rose thought. They were stockier than any horse Rose had seen before, and taller, and they had thick grey frizzy manes and grey bristles on their chins that made them look like they had beards.

Everyone had to admit they were indeed beautiful. All except Bubbles. Firstly he was annoyed that he was facing backwards when everybody else was taking in the sight of the beasts.

"Hello? What are you all looking at? All I can see is trees! This is what I get for watching your backs, is it? Ignored?! Great! Thanks a lot! Note to self: don't bother bringing up the rear in future!"

Eventually Rose turned round to let him see the gorgeous animals. "See? Aren't they beautiful?"

"Meh," huffed Bubbles, unimpressed. "I suppose everyone has different tastes."

Right on cue one of the horses did a poo in front of them.

"See? Look at that poo. It's splattered all over the place. My poos are neat and tidy and nobody calls me beautiful!"

Everyone wisely ignored Bubbles and walked among the horses.

Rose marvelled at the great beasts. She watched them chewing the grass and breathing out plumes of steam from their nostrils like dragons. It reminded her of the bit in the *Jurassic Park* movies when the kids meet the dinosaurs. Or of a book she once read about a little girl meeting a unicorn. These weren't dinosaurs or unicorns but she was pretty sure she'd never get this up close and personal with wild animals in the modern world.

"Thanks for showing us these, Merdyn," she said to her old friend. "It's a sight I'll remember for ever."

"Oh, I didn't bringeth us here to look at them. We're going to ride them."

Arthur was delighted at this. Fun Merdyn was back again! "Yes!!!" he cried. "I was starting to get foot rot with all this walking."

Rose was less pleased. "But I don't know how to ride a horse. Especially a wild one with no reins or saddle or anything."

"I'm with Rose on this one," said Bubbles unsurprisingly. "Pigs of any sort do not ride horses."

"Thou art always welcome to run as I do," Wolf sneered, knowing full well a guinea pig's running range is only about fifteen metres.

"See, there be an example of thinking in the negative," the wise wizard remarked. "It's as old as the battle between light and dark. Ye are going to rideth these horses all right. We shall be at Vanheldon's fort in no time. They will not be expecting us so soon. And so we shall have the element of surprise on our side."

"Sounds good to me! Let's ride!" enthused Arthur and rushed towards a tarpan.

The horse immediately whinnied, pawed its hoofs in the air and bolted for the horizon.

"Patience, Arthur. Thou cannot just hop atop a wild horse," Merdyn said. "Which is why Rose is going to tame them with her taming spell."

Rose reached into her herb belt for some lavender, the perfect choice for a calming spell, but Merdyn stopped her.

"*Without* using any herbs," he added, winking at Rose.

"But, Merdyn, I can't do that," said Rose.

"Yes, thou can. Thou needst to learn to believeth in thyself, Rose. But fear not, I'm going to teach thee how to harness the power of light. Right now."

Rose was confused. "Right now? But it's night-time."

"Light is always around us," said Merdyn. "We merely need to find it. Now close thine eyes and thinketh about the Earth. Thinketh about the ground beneath thy feet. The energy connecting all nature. The mountains, the trees, the grass, the moon, the stars are all one." Rose closed her eyes. "Now summoneth the light, and feeleth the light gather and glow in thy heart."

Rose tried to feel a light in her heart but after a few minutes she was getting nothing. Then she thought of her mother and the love she had for her, and Kris – how much she missed him. And her dad. She thought of Bubbles too and Merdyn. She felt her heart grow and, yes, through her eyelids she could see a faint glow . . .

Merdyn saw it too. Rose was summoning the light! Her whole being was starting to glow with a yellowy hue. The others saw it as well.

"That's it, Rose! Thou can do it! Concentrate. Feel the light. Feel the light of love and say thy spell."

Rose did as he said.

"ANIMA TRUFONMEN KEEPICALMICUS!"

She pointed a finger towards one of the wild horses and light streamed from her finger, inching towards the horse, stretching, getting closer and closer . . . She was almost there when – ARGH! It faded. Rose had lost her train of thought and the light had disappeared.

She cursed herself. "I couldn't do it."

But Merdyn smiled proudly. "I have *never* seen anyone do so well on their first try. Well done, Rose."

Even Bubbles was impressed. "You know you went all yellow then for a second. I mean, I'm yellow all the time but . . . again, no one gives me credit for it."

Merdyn then performed the taming spell on three of the tarpans and Rose (with Bubbles in her backpack, his eyes closed), Arthur and Merdyn climbed on the backs of the magnificent beasts.

"Just holdeth on to the mane, Rose," Arthur suggested. As a king, he was highly trained in horse riding. "Left or right will steereth it, push forward to go faster, pulleth back to stop. Be firm with thy movements. Horses can sense fear. If thou art scared, the horse will be scared."

"I'm not scared," said Rose, feeling much more positive now.

Bubbles yelped from Rose's backpack. "*I'm* scared!"

"Thankfully, thou don't count," Arthur said to the guinea pig. "Yah!"

Arthur and Merdyn pushed their horses forward, while Wolf sped ahead of them on foot to lead them to the safest track.

"Yah!" said Rose, copying them, and pushed the mane of her horse forward.

WHOOSH! It took off.

"*Whhooooooaohhhhmyyyygadsbudliiiikjnnnnnssss!*" she cried as she felt the wind in her frizzy hair and the mighty horse galloping strongly beneath her.

"Whhhaaaat's haaaapenniiiiing?!" shrieked Bubbles

from behind her, his eyes still closed.

"I'm riding a flipping horse, that's what!" yelled Rose, unable to contain her joy.

If she wasn't missing Mum,
and Kris wasn't facing strife,
This would definitely be
the best moment of her life.

CHAPTER TWENTY-ONE

MUCH VAUNTED BADDIES AND SUCH HAUNTED VALLEYS!

Vanheldon had been stewing over what Druilla had said about his daughter, and then one day it came to a head – over stew!

Vanheldon had entered the main room of the fort to hassle Druilla about her plans to kill Merdyn – his patience was growing thin – when he saw Vanhessa feeding Kris his morning pottage. Not only was she feeding him gently, using a piece of cloth to dab away any spillage from his chin, but the pottage looked different. Usually it had bones sticking out of it and lumps and greasy bits. But this stew was smooth and completely non-lumpy.

Vanheldon broke off his march towards Druilla, who was again doodling on her slate while sitting by the sink, to speak with his daughter.

"What be this?!" he demanded, grabbing the bowl from Vanhessa's hand and stirring his finger in it. "'Tis mush."

Vanhessa seemed to blush. "Kris – I meaneth, the prisoner – does not liketh bones, so I taketh them out for him. It tasteth much better that way if thou would wish to tryeth it."

But Vanheldon didn't wish to try it. Instead he threw the bowl against a wall, creating a circle of mushy pottage on it, like a piece of modern art.

"A private word, daughter," he said ominously and gestured for her to join him at the fireplace. She did so.

"What in the name of Gadsbudlikins art thou doing? Laughing and joking with the prisoner? Removing bones from his food? Oh, he does not like bones, does he? Then giveth him more!! He is bait for Merdyn, and nothing else."

"And when we have killed Merdyn? What then?" asked Vanhessa, trying to keep all emotion from her voice.

"Then we have no need for him any more," her father replied in a matter-of-fact way.

"Meaning what, Father?"

Vanheldon was angry with his daughter for pushing him like this. "Don't maketh me spell it out, Vanhessa, because for a start I cannot read nor write!"

"Father," began Vanhessa thoughtfully, "are we the baddies?"

Vanheldon's brain could not fathom such a strange question. "What art thou talking about, 'baddies'?"

"I mean, the villains. Are we the bad people?"

Vanheldon thought for a second. It was perhaps the first time he'd considered this question in his life. "Well, no. No, we are not the baddies."

"Art thou sure, Father, because we have done some bad things. We have killed and maimed and tortured people."

"Aye, but in war it is either kill or be killed."

Vanhessa stared at him with her green eyes. "Aye, but usually we start the war, Father."

Vanheldon poked the fire vigorously with a handy stick. "This is untrue, Vanhessa. The Celts attacked us first!"

"Nay, we attacked the Romans," countered Vanhessa.

"Aye, but . . . they invaded our country way before thou were born. We were just putting right a wrong."

"I know but we did not need to smash all their artworks and frescoes and statues. In the future they call people who destroy other people's property 'vandals'. They name them after US!"

"That does not make us baddies, Vanhessa!"

"And then there be our clothings?" she said, looking them both up and down. "Furs of dead animals. Dead rats. Bears' teeth?"

Vanheldon started to squirm. "Most of those animals died of natural causes."

"No, they did not!" Vanhessa snapped. "These teeth?" she said, pointing to the bigger teeth on her necklace, "are from General Brown, my pet bear."

"Oh, not this again!' moaned her father, exasperated. "That bear caught a brain disease and went mad. It needed to be put down."

"It was winter and thou were hungry!"

"A person needeth meat!"

"Kris says in the future some people do not

eateth meat!"

"What? That is absurd. Anyway, eating meat does not maketh us baddies."

"Then what about the name of our fort?"

"What about it?"

"Fort Doom."

"'Tis a nice name for a house!"

"'Tis the name of a baddie's house!"

Vanheldon finally lost his temper. "That's enough of this!!" he bellowed. "Thou art my daughter and thou will supporteth me in my efforts to killeth my enemies." Vanhessa went to reply but her father wasn't finished. "Merdyn destroyed our entire army, remember?"

Vanhessa was stopped in her tracks. She did remember.

"Exactly . . ." said Vanheldon, knowing he'd finally scored a point. "So if thou wanteth to talk about baddies, maybe we should talketh about Merdyn the Wild and anyone who supporteth him? Including the prisoner!"

Vanhessa bowed her head.

"Now cometh with me while I talketh to Druilla."

"Yes, Father." She followed him to confront

the wicked witch.

"Druilla," he began firmly, trying to reassert his authority, "we demandeth to know the plan to dispatch with Merdyn the Pain in the Backside! They now rideth the tarpans! Those horses never tire; they runneth on fresh air. They shall be upon us in no time. And thou just – just sitteth there drawing on thy slate like a . . . like a fopdoodle!*"

Druilla sighed and showed him what she'd been working on. It was a map of Europe. She pointed to a trail leading to Vanheldon's fort.

"They are travelling this route, on the grasslands. Merdyn will not travel by air or water as he knows my magic can reach him. The land is too thick even for dark magic to taketh a hold. But if they are to reacheth us, they will *have* to cross here, and this is no ordinary land." She tapped the slate where she had drawn a skeleton.

Vanheldon knew the place immediately. He trembled. "Skeleton Valley?"

"Skeleton Valley," the witch repeated.

---

*Fopdoodle is one of my absolute favorite words of old. It means a lazy, idle person. Some think over time the word morphed into the Americanism "dude". Thanks for reading this footnote, carry on reading, dude!

"What be Skeleton Valley, Father?" asked Vanhessa.

"'Tis a place where the ancients sacrificed animals to please the gods," the ex-Vandal king told his daughter. "And not just animals. Enemy prisoners, their children sometimes, anything to please the heavens. 'Tis a dreadful place where no man or woman travels willingly."

"Except me," Druilla butted in proudly. "'Tis a place I once called home."

"Thou did *liveth* in Skeleton Valley?!" Vanheldon thought a mouse must have got stuck in his ear again. "No one could possibly liveth there. 'Tis like the gates of hell."

"One person's hell be another person's heaven," Druilla reasoned. "I have been on a journey to harness the power of darkness. It has taken me many places; Skeleton Valley is but one. The place and I have a special connection. Merdyn cannot be protected by his precious light there. In Skeleton Valley we shall striketh again. And I have a very exciting new spell."

Now Vanheldon smiled. Finally he could understand Druilla's plan. "Yeees. Now I shall have revenge on Merdyn!"

But something was bothering Druilla. In the back of her crystal ball she could still see two mysterious people following in the rescue team's footsteps.

Destiny was close,
she could smell it with her nose.
But who was it
that lurked in the shadows?

CHAPTER TWENTY-TWO

SPIRITUAL HOLES
AND
RESTLESS SOULS

Riding a tarpan is about as good as it gets for an animal lover like Rose. This was an experience she could never have in the modern world. For a start, there are very few wild horses left in the world*.

And for a finish, even if you could find a wild horse, you couldn't ride it with this sort of abandon. You would soon encounter a road or a fence or be chased from someone's property.

Here in 521 in northern Europe it was possible to ride for days without any restrictions whatsoever. And the tarpans were so strong! They could leap over fallen trees, wade through rivers, clamber over mountains.

---

*In fact, there are hardly any truly wild horses left in the world. There are some that roam free in western USA and Australia but these originate from domesticated horses that have gone feral. The only truly wild horses left are the Przewalski's, which are native to the steppes of central Asia. They nearly went extinct like the tarpan but are making a comeback thanks to conservation efforts. Way to go, conservation efforts!!

And what beauty Rose saw!

Imagine a planet without cities or motorways, without so much as a brick house! Just pure untouched nature. Vast, dense forests untouched by loggers. Pristine grasslands that swayed in the wind like hair in a shampoo advert. Rivers and waterfalls that flowed with cool clear water from the mountains, not a sewage pipe or a plastic bottle in sight. Rose knew how lucky she was to have seen this, and mentally photographed it all so she could tell people just how magnificent it was.

Of course, as much as Rose loved riding the wild horse, Bubbles hated it. While Rose marvelled at the sights and sounds of the Dark Ages, Bubbles stayed in her backpack listing the reasons he DIDN'T like the Dark Ages.

1. No organic muesli.
2. No cars to get around.
3. No central heating.
4. Too many wolves.
5. No organic muesli.

Bubbles was mightily relieved then when the tarpans came to an abrupt halt at the entrance to a mysterious-looking valley shrouded in shadows.

"Whoa there!" said Merdyn when his horse started shying away as he tried to urge it forward. The other horses didn't want to enter the sinister valley either. Wolf had been ahead and he came back with an explanation.

"I believeth this is the place they calleth Skeleton Valley," he said to Merdyn.

Merdyn was gobsmacked. "I thought that was a myth."

"Why do I not like the sound of Skeleton Valley?" said Rose nervously.

"For a very good reason. When the Romans were forced out of northern Europe they left behind a hole—" Merdyn began.

"What? Like a rabbit hole?" Bubbles enquired, finally popping his head out of Rose's backpack.

"No, more a spiritual hole."

"Thou wouldn't understand." No prizes for guessing who said this in a haughty voice.

"People had nothing to believe in," Merdyn continued,

ignoring Wolf. "And so they invented gods. A god for this, a god for that. And, pertinent to this story, a god for crops. One year, when his crops were failing, a farmer sacrificed his goat in this valley. The next day the rains came and his crops were saved. Since then when anybody needed to ask something of the gods they would come and push some poor creature off the cliffs into this valley. Many goats, sheep, horses, chickens, even human beings have met their end in this place, and it is said their restless souls still walketh the valley bed."

"OK, that's a good reason to go round it then," said Bubbles, hoping that would be the end of it.

"We must passeth through the valley or it is three more days added to our journey," Wolf informed the gang. "Get through here and we shall be at Vanheldon's fort by tomorrow morn."

"Well, there's nothing else for it—" said Rose.

"Yep, I agree," Bubbles cut in. "Three more days it is."

"No, Bubbles. I was going to say we have no choice but to go through it."

"I agreeth with lovely Rose," said Arthur, getting down from his tarpan. "And if the tarpans won't pass through, then we must goeth on foot."

Bubbles piped up again. "Hello?! You do know what 'restless souls' means, right? It literally means ghosts. OK?"

Merdyn backtracked. "I didn't say there *were* ghosts. I said, *it is said* that their restless souls—"

Bubbles was very angry now. "Yeah. By people who have *seen* the ghosts! Hello!? The place is literally, actually in real life called Skeleton Valley!"

"We can't lose any more time, Bubbles," said Rose. "We have to think of Kris. The quicker we get to him, the bigger the chance that he's still alive and we can rescue him and all go home. We *must* go through the valley."

And with that Rose climbed down from her horse, gave him a kiss on the nose to say thank you and watched him race away. Merdyn did the same (but without the kiss on the nose). And our intrepid heroes entered Skeleton Valley.

Bubbles shook his head and zipped himself back into Rose's backpack. A voice was heard from within.

"This is a bad idea," he said.

*"Just remember I said not to go.
I ain't afraid to say I told you so."*

CHAPTER TWENTY-THREE

FROM THE DEPTHS OF HELL COMES A SPECIAL SPELL

Druilla watched with glee as Merdyn and the others took their first steps into Skeleton Valley. Kris strained to see the crystal ball from where he was tied to the stake. Vanhessa joined her father at the giant stone sink.

The evil witch then delved into her clothes once more and pulled out a small bottle with black liquid inside it. She poured it into the sink. She poured and she poured. Even though the bottle was small, the liquid it contained filled the entire sink to the brim with black oily soup.

"I've been looking forward to this." She smirked and let out a cackle. Then she lifted the sleeves of her dress to her elbows and let her hands enter the water.

What is she up to now? Kris asked himself. But whatever it was there was nothing he could do about it. His magic had been taken from him. He was helpless to prevent whatever horrors were about to befall his poor sister and their gang.

Back in Skeleton Valley, Kris's rescue team made their way carefully through the infamous gorge. It had been formed millions of years ago by an ancient glacier that had cleft a V-shaped swathe through the land.

The dry riverbed was covered in huge rocks and boulders that had been left behind when the glacier melted. The sides of the valley rose nearly a hundred metres to the top of the cliffs where the desperate farmers and hopeful traders used to offer up sacrifices to the gods.

Rose certainly felt the valley lived up to its name, because among the huge boulders were countless skeletons of dead animals and humans that had been picked clean of meat by vultures and other carrion birds. These scavenger birds still hung around, evidently hoping for a new victim to pounce on. But it didn't look like the valley had been used for years.

"What's it like?" asked Bubbles from deep within

Rose's backpack. "Is it bad?"

"I would just stay in the bag if I were you, Bubbles," said Rose, knowing her pet wouldn't have the stomach for the sight of all these bones.

"This place does not scare me," claimed Arthur, treading without care over the old bones.

Merdyn frowned at him. "Remember, Arthur, we must always have respect for the dead. Never forgetteth that."

"Yeah, yeah," huffed Arthur. "It's only a ship load of old cows and sheep and—"

Just then, Wolf stopped, pointed his tail and held up his paw. This was the universal wolf pack sign for everybody to stop. The gang looked at each other for a second, wondering what the problem was.

They soon found out!

Very slowly all the giant boulders immediately ahead of them, about forty in total, each the size of a suitcase, started to move of their own accord!

The huge stones shifted and turned and started to arrange themselves to form two structures, each with five lines of three or four boulders strung together. The structures planted themselves in the ground and stood up like fingers, where they were joined by a larger slab that connected them.

"I standeth corrected," muttered Arthur under his breath. "It's only a ship load of old cows and sheep and . . . two giant *hands*!"

The boulders had arranged themselves to look like two huge skeleton hands fully six metres high!

Merdyn knew this to be the same dark magic that they'd experienced with the salamanders. But this trick was even better!

"Standeth back, children! Let me dealeth with this," he ordered Rose and Arthur, and stepped towards the bony (or rather *stony*) hands, brandishing his staff, Thundarian. "This be dark magic indeed!"

Back in the castle, Vanheldon hopped from one foot to the other in sheer excitement as he watched Druilla move her

hands under the water.

Kris realised what was happening. What Druilla did with her hands under water would be mirrored by the stony hands in Skeleton Valley. It was like remote-control hands! Like some weird computer game. Rose and the others were in big trouble. And there was nothing he could do about it.

"Now," said Druilla evilly, "let us squisheth them like the cockroaches they are!"

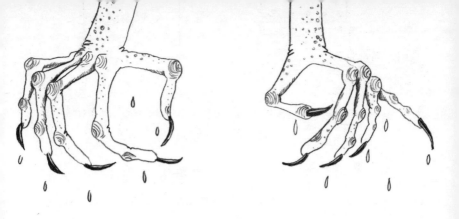

In Skeleton Valley Merdyn dodged a stony hand as it tried to swipe at him. He thumped his staff on the ground. "Light, cometh to me!" he cried, and a blinding light struck the elegant eagle atop Thundarian. Using the light to power him, Merdyn chanted the levitation spell –

"TRILLIUM, PEUMUS, LEVITATO-US!"

– and rose up in the air just as the second hand flew towards him in a fist.

Wolf ran in between the fingers at great speed, barking. The hand swiped at him like you or I trying to catch a moth, but Wolf was super agile and just kept moving, frustrating the flailing fingers.

Merdyn threw a tremendous bolt of lightning at one of the hands, exploding it into pieces.

"HOLCUS CRACKAJACKA!"

"Yes!!" cried Rose from behind the rock. "In your face, hands!"

Arthur looked at her, confused.

"It's an, er . . . modern expression," she explained.

But her and Arthur's joy turned to horror as the stones slowly reassembled. It was like watching them being scattered but in reverse, like they were attracting each other magnetically. Soon they were exactly as they had been *before* the lightning strike.

Merdyn swallowed and looked at Wolf. It was a look that said "We've won some battles, thee and I, but nothing like this . . ."

Suddenly – WHAM! – the reassembled hand thwacked a stunned Merdyn in his side and sent him hurtling into a rock. THUMP!

"Merdyn!" cried Rose.

Wolf howled and snapped at the hands, who swiped at him this way and that. Finally one of the hands swatted him aside too and he yelped as he struck the cliff face. AWOOOOOO!!

In the castle Vanheldon was like the kid at the party who'd scoffed too many sweets. He was foaming at the mouth and shouting for Druilla to "Finisheth him! Finisheth Merdyn!"

Druilla smiled and turned a finger towards the stricken wizard.

In Skeleton Valley Rose watched helplessly as a giant bony finger lifted above Merdyn, who clearly had broken his leg and couldn't move.

"How are you with that sword?" she asked Arthur, who suddenly seemed bashful.

"Good in practice, but I have never used it in the field of battle."

"Well, now's the time to start . . ." said Rose. Then she ran out from behind the rock towards the hands. She reached into her belt and threw some herbs and shouted,

"GELIDA GLACIA FROSTORA!"

– sending a frost spell that encased one of the hands in ice.

The other hand tried to swipe at her but Rose threw more herbs and chanted,

"TRILLIUM PEUMUS LEVITATO-US,"

causing her to levitate just in time and the hand sailed harmlessly underneath her.

"Wow," said Arthur to himself from behind the rock. "I think I have found out what 'cool' meaneth."

The frozen hand then burst out of its frosty shell and both hands tried to crush Rose.

THUMP, THUMP!

But Rose, without thinking it through, leaped on to a stone finger and kept leaping. She didn't need a spell for this, she just recalled how she'd crossed a river on a school trip using stepping stones. The only way to succeed was to keep going! She bounded from stone to stone to stone with great speed as the hands tried to grasp her. They just couldn't keep track of her.

In the castle Druilla was astonished. She'd never seen such bravery in one so young.

She knew that Rose
was a special W-blood,
But why had no one told her
she was so good?

CHAPTER TWENTY-FOUR

ALLIES NEED TO RALLY IN SKELETON VALLEY!

Kris watched Rose battling the giant hands and was filled with pride for his little sister.

"Go, Rose!" he yelled.

This was a mistake, however, as Druilla hurled a spell at him, **"FINCANTUS! SILENCIO! LIPSEALUS!"** and suddenly Kris no longer had a mouth.

"Mmmmmffff," he said.

Druilla turned her attention back to the girl, but she couldn't rid her from her fingers. Rose was like a ladybird crawling over her hand that she just couldn't shake off.

Arthur finally realised he needed to stop hiding and

do something.

Seeing Merdyn stricken was distressing. He might be a judgy old mentor, but he was HIS judgy old mentor. He took a deep breath, pulled Excalibur from its sheath and ran towards the hands, swishing and slashing.

Thankfully, he was pretty cool himself. Rose could hardly believe her eyes as Arthur used Excalibur to cut THROUGH the stones. One by one the magnificent sword cleft the rocks in two, forcing them to lose their power.

Rose was running round the stony fingers like something out of a martial arts movie and Arthur was slicing them to pieces with Excalibur! They were winning!

"Rose!" cried Arthur. "I think I have found something else to focus on!" He beamed proudly before nearly being decapitated by a flying finger.

"That's great, Arthur!" shouted Rose. "But let's not celebrate yet, eh?"

At the castle Druilla was furious as Rose cast spell after spell to outwit her.

"BARBARIUM INVISIBLATIS!"

Rose cried, becoming invisible and therefore impossible to catch.

"TRANSFORMUS BOWLUS BALLUS!"

she yelled – one of Merdyn's favourite spells from modern times – and became a bowling ball, careering into a hand and sending the boulders scattering like bowling pins.

"No!! they cannot beat me! No one can beat me!" Druilla screamed. "Vanheldon? Put in thy hands!"

Vanheldon smiled, only too happy to help. He lifted his sleeves up and plunged his hands into the dark liquid in the sink.

Kris groaned. This made it a very unfair fight. He caught Vanhessa's eye. She was looking uncomfortable.

Rose and Arthur had finally seen off the stone hands, which now lay in pieces. Rose had darted around like a firefly and Arthur had followed with his sword, his confidence with Excalibur growing as he swished and slashed the boulders in two, then four parts. But their joy was short-lived.

"Er . . . you might want to look behind you," said Bubbles from her backpack. He'd only just been brave enough to open his eyes because it seemed like the fight was over.

Rose gulped. There were now TWO NEW HANDS of stone coming towards them. Not only that, the previously defeated hands were slowly coming back together as before. Soon Rose and Arthur were going to have to battle FOUR HANDS, and Rose's herbs were running out.

"Our only chance is to run," figured Rose, panting.

Arthur grimaced. "But Merdyn and Wolf, they are stricken . . ."

Rose looked at Merdyn – he was sitting against a rock in agony. He clearly couldn't concentrate on magic while he was in such pain. Wolf was trying to limp towards them, but he was lame too. Rose cursed herself as she looked at the empty herb pouches on her belt. If only she didn't need to rely on her herb belt! If only she could use the power of light! If only she weren't the worst W-blood who had ever lived!

"We've done it once, Arthur. Let's do it again. But twice as fast!" Rose jumped on the new hands and started leaping from finger to finger. As before, Arthur followed, slicing the boulders this way and that. Rose and Arthur were becoming quite the team. But battling four hands was too much for them.

Trying to make an impossible leap from one hand to

another, Rose fell and landed among the skeleton bones of an old bison.

One of the stony hands curled into a fist and plummeted down towards Rose. It was going to flatten her for sure.

"Nooooooooooooooooooooooo!" yelled Bubbles and closed his eyes but –

SWISH- THUMP!

– Arthur pulled Rose out of harm's way at the last second.

Back at the castle, Vanheldon's patience was wearing thin.

"Thee! Daughter!" he hissed at Vanhessa, not even bothering to use her name. "Thrust thy hands in here. If thou joinest us, they will be dead in the blink of an eye!"

Vanhessa hesitated.

"Do as I order, daughter!" he barked again and Vanhessa walked slowly to the sink.

Kris watched in horror. If Vanhessa joined in, Rose and Arthur would have SIX hands to defeat and that would surely prove too much! Unable to speak, his eyes spoke to Vanhessa instead – *please don't do it!*

Vanhessa knew it was time to choose. There were goodies and baddies and she knew which side she was on. She had known since she was born. It was her destiny.

Vanhessa rolled up her sleeves and bent over the sink. Kris closed his eyes and prayed. But he should have kept them open . . .

For instead of lowering her hands in the water and helping her father, Vanhessa placed her hands *under* the sink and heaved!

"Vanhessa!" her father bellowed. "What art thou doing, girl?"

The sink was enormous, as big as a bathtub and made of solid rock. It must have weighed two tons but the strength of this Vandal girl was equal to it.

"Hmnnnnnaaaaarghhhhh!" she grunted, and the sink rolled forward and the dark-magic water spilled on to the floor and down the cracks in the stones.

Druilla's eyes blazed with anger. But it was nothing compared to that of Vanheldon.

> *Stunned, he turned upon his daughter*
> *with fury.*
> *Punishment would soon follow,*
> *without a jury!*

CHAPTER TWENTY-FIVE

BUBBLES WAS RIGHT ... AND FACING ANOTHER FIGHT!

Rose and Arthur were battered and bruised and almost out of ideas when suddenly the four hands mysteriously collapsed into lifeless, scattered rocks once more.

"I hate to say I told you this was a bad idea," Bubbles piped up from his backpack position, "but I actually literally said 'This is a bad idea'."

Rose and Arthur looked at each other for a second, exhausted and relieved, before rushing to Merdyn and Wolf.

"Merdyn! Are you OK? Where does it hurt?" asked Rose.

Merdyn groaned. "My leg," he murmured. "My head."

Arthur had checked Wolf's leg. "We should get out of here," he said to Rose. "Let us carryeth them. They cannot walk. We must hasten before the hands returneth once more."

Arthur carried his mentor and Rose carried Wolf half a mile or so to the other side of the infamous Valley. Once there, an exhausted Rose and Arthur put down their injured charges and set up camp for the night.

Merdyn took Rose's hand. "My powers fadeth, Rose. I knoweth not why. But thou must help me. Thou mendest animals in thy shed. Thou can fixeth Wolf. And the same spell may worketh on this old fool."

Rose had never seen Merdyn like this before. Usually he was so powerful; he had the answers to everything. But now he was relying on her.

She remembered the spell she'd used to fix the broken leg of a parrot in her clinic (it seemed like such a long time ago – or rather, a long time in the future!) and went to fetch the required herbs from the forest nearby. She found milk thistle and St John's wort and tried the spell on Wolf's broken leg and it worked. But it wasn't so successful on Merdyn. He was still pale and weak. Nevertheless, he could stand up now and walk around, albeit with the aid of his staff. Rose was upset to see her usually ebullient friend so frail and feeble, but at least he was alive.

Arthur collected ingredients and made everyone pottage over the fire that night as they reflected on the day's traumatic events.

"Well done, Rose." Merdyn spoke weakly. "And thee, Arthur. Thou art finally learning. Thou may maketh a great king yet."

Arthur was so excited he was almost bouncing out of his armour.

"'May'? 'May'? I WILL make a great king. Oh, thou should have seen us, Merdyn!" he trilled. "We were a great team! Rose was doing her magic, and me with Excalibur, SWISH, SWOSH, SWISH. Wow. We were pretty COOL!"

"I'm sure it was 'cool'," said Merdyn, trying to smile. "It is good to knoweth my two disciples can worketh together so well. If t'were not for ye, Wolf and I would surely be dead."

Rose could see that something was on Merdyn's mind. "What's worrying you, Merdyn?" she asked the

great wizard.

Merdyn laughed. "Good old Rose, thou could always readeth me like one of thy books." Merdyn shuffled uncomfortably before speaking again. "We are almost there. The other side of that forest lies Vanheldon's fort. There we will findeth Kris and I hope we will getteth thee and he home, Rose."

"But . . ." prompted Rose.

Merdyn carried on. "But I do not liketh what I am feeling as we get close. I knoweth that we faceth a great battle when we get there. And we should be ready to do whatever it taketh to win. But winneth we must. My powers, they groweth weak. My light. It fadeth. If we letteth the darkness win then the light would be gone from the world for ever. Do thou understandeth, Rose?"

"I think so, Merdyn," she replied. She was also worried about what they would find at Vanheldon's fort. But as long as Merdyn was with them she figured they would find a way. He had the answer to everything, after all. They just needed some rest.

"Well, I don't know about anyone else but I think I deserve some food," said Bubbles as he tucked into a bowl of pottage. "If you can call this food!"

"I don't recall thee getting involved in the action today, Bubbles," said Wolf, who was happily gnawing on a meaty bone that Rose had found for him.

"Not involved in the action?" cried Bubbles. "You were the one lying down while I literally had Rose's back."

"Hmm . . ." said the pompous Wolf. "Being *on* someone's back is not the same as *having* someone's back."

And so the group were subject to another bickering

session from Bubbles and Wolf. But this night they were glad of it.

> *The Wolf and Bubbles*
> *bickering show*
> *Took their minds*
> *off the dread of tomorrow.*

CHAPTER TWENTY-SIX

FREEDOM IS SNATCHED
AND A
NEW PLAN IS HATCHED

Immediately after Vanhessa had toppled over the stone sink, her father had tied his daughter's wrists and tethered her to the same wooden stake as Kris.

"Please, Father, she is corrupting thee!" Vanhessa started to protest, but—

"FINCANTUS! SILENCIO! LIPSEALUS!"

Druilla sealed her lips up too. Now she and Kris were mouthless prisoners.

"I knoweth not what cameth over her," seethed the Vandal king, his voice cracking under the weight of disappointment. "The boy must putteth a spell on her."

"Nonsense!" hissed Druilla. "I have takeneth the boy's magic. He is nothing but a mortal husk! However

. . ." She put herself close to Kris's face. He stared back at her bravely. "Hmm. He may have putteth a spell on her in some other way?"

Vanheldon was pitch-kettled*.

"What do thou meaneth?"

"I mean, perhaps she is in love with the thin-eyebrowed creature?"

Vanhessa blushed and her father erupted in protestation.

"My daughter loveth no one but her father and war!"

"Then how do thou explaineth her treachery?" Druilla scolded not unreasonably.

"I knoweth not," replied a downcast Vanheldon.

"But thou knowest now she cannot be trusted. So asketh thine idle guards to take these fools to the dungeons where they cannot cause any more mischief."

Vanhessa looked at her father pleadingly but he just stared back at her with disdain.

"Guards!" he shouted, and his two remaining soldiers ran in and stood to attention.

---

*Confused. Come on, you have GOT to read the previous book!

"Taketh these two to the tower," he ordered. The two guards untied Kris and Vanhessa from the stake. They tried to protest but their voiceless mouths could say nothing but "MMMMUUUHMMMMUUUH!" as they were taken to Fort Doom's tower, above which the giant wooden bullhorns poked into the air. The tower served as its prison and Kris and Vanhessa were dragged up the rickety stairs and hurled into one of the thick-walled rooms and bolted in.

When they were gone Vanheldon turned to Druilla. "I understandeth not my daughter." He shook his head as he spoke. "She has changed lately."

"Children are like that," the evil witch replied with a knowing look in her eye. "They are all sweetness and light and then they *STAB THEE IN THE BACK*!" As she said this she stamped the ground with such force that the whole building shuddered.

But Vanheldon agreed with her. What was the point in having children if they didn't do exactly as their parents bid them?

"Do thou knoweth what she asked me yesterday?!"

Vanheldon carried on, wanting to get some things off his chest. "She said 'Are we the baddies?' 'ARE WE THE BADDIES?' Can thou believeth that?"

"And what did thou sayeth?" Druilla enquired.

"Well, I said, 'No.'"

"And thou would be right!" said Druilla cheerfully. "Which is precisely why we are going to let Merdyn and the rest of his pathetic crew marcheth right into Fort Doom!"

This last statement caught Vanheldon by surprise.

"Er . . . sayeth what now? I thought we were going to killeth them?"

"But that is what a so-called baddie would doeth, is it not?"

Vanheldon was very confused now. "Er, well, yes, but . . ." He couldn't understand what she meant. All he knew was killing and war, but he couldn't admit that lest he also admit that he was a baddie. Thankfully, Druilla helped him out.

"We're going to let them walketh in here because we have a higher purpose," she told him. "We believeth in a world without fighting and war."

"Do we?"

"Yes. Think about it. Why did thou have to fighteth the Romans?"

This one was easy. "Ah! Because they invaded our lands first."

"Exactly! But if there were only one ruler. One person that the world bowed down to. Whose power was unquestioned. That everybody obeyed. There would be no more need for invasions, would there? There would be no need for war and fighting. There would be peace."

"Right . . ." said Vanheldon, "and . . . that one ruler is . . .?"

"Thee and me," answered Druilla.

"Rrrrrright." Vanheldon narrowed his eyes as his brain worked overtime. "But that be *two* people."

"Yes, but we thinketh as one, do we not?"

Vanheldon wasn't sure they did, but she was an evil witch, so he kept this concern to himself. Instead he wanted to go back to the "letting his arch-enemy march into his fort bit".

"Listen," Druilla explained, "Merdyn is the most powerful wizard in the known world. His descendant Rose showeth great promise too. If we letteth them come here, I can stealeth their magic and become the most magical person who ever liveth . . ."

Vanheldon was getting it. "I see! *Then* we killeth them?"

"If thou likest," muttered Druilla. "Once I have their magic I really do not care. But here be the best bit – did thou seest the sword that the fool King Arthur wieldeth in Skeleton Valley?"

"The one so shiny it twinkleth like the stars?" the Vandal king remembered helpfully.

"Yes, that one. *That* is Excalibur. And whosoe'er holds Excalibur is the rightful king of England – the English madeth that rule so they must standeth by it."

"Ooh! That could be me!" Vanheldon rejoiced, suddenly seeing the benefit of the new plan.

"Exactly!" agreed Druilla. "With my powers and that sword there will only be one ruler . . . '

"Two," corrected Vanheldon.

"*Two* rulers to unify the whole world. And, believe me, when I—"

"We . . ." Vanheldon corrected again.

"When *we* rule the whole world," Druilla continued, building to a crescendo, a dark scowl now etched on her face, "I assure thee, Vanheldon, there will be no more *ungrateful children to bother us . . .*"

> *Now, dear reader,*
> *it might be just me,*
> *But a world ruled by Druilla*
> *does not fill me with glee.*

CHAPTER TWENTY-SEVEN

TARNISH EXPLAINED AND AN ANIMAL NAMED

The next day, Rose, Merdyn, Arthur, Bubbles and Wolf set off for Vanheldon's fort. Rose and Arthur took it in turns to help Merdyn as he was still limping badly.

They were expecting a few more surprises of the "massive fire salamander" or "giant stone hands" variety but none were forthcoming, which led Merdyn to worry even more about the trap that was awaiting them.

They knew that they were getting close to Fort Doom when they started to see the pathway lined with wooden stakes, on top of which were skewered gruesome items like tigers' heads and dead rats.

Bubbles gulped when he saw these. "Once again I demand a full enquiry into the way these people treat animals."

"Do be quiet, thou undersized pig," Wolf groaned.

"They treat all life with disdain. That skull over there, for example, is from a bear."

Bubbles looked at the dead bear's head but didn't see this as any reason to stop complaining. "Then let the bears call for their own enquiry. Every animal can speak for itself."

As he said this he realised it wasn't exactly true. He ought to have said "every animal can speak for itself IF IT HAS AN ENCHANTED PINECONE ON ITS HEAD." But he couldn't be bothered, and anyway the moment had passed.

The gang reached the crest of a hill and there they saw, perched on the next hill, the home of the ex-Vandal king Vanheldon, Fort Doom!

Huge dark clouds hovered above the giant wooden bullhorns of the tower. Rose saw Merdyn look at them and shiver. As they got closer, she saw that the trees and plants had become withered and black, and when they crossed a bridge she saw the river had completely dried up, leaving a blackened riverbed with dead fish rotting here and there.

"What happened here?" Rose asked Merdyn. "It's like

something has killed all the wildlife."

"'Tis the Tarnish," Merdyn answered in a tone that Rose did not like at all.

"I take it the Tarnish is not a good thing?"

"Not in the least."

"What is it?"

"It is something of a mystery. All I knoweth is that wherever dark magic resides, the Tarnish will follow. It strangleth nature. It killeth anything that lives in its path. Plants, trees, flowers, animals, even humans will choketh in its wake. Someone or something in that dread fort is creating it. And we must stop them."

"Vanheldon?" wondered Rose aloud.

"No, no," Merdyn answered with conviction. "It is the person who helpeth Vanheldon. Or *useth* him perhaps. It matters not. What matters is that we stoppeth them. It will not be easy but stoppeth them we must. We must be ready to fight with our lives."

"I'm ready!" proclaimed a confident Arthur, and he twirled his sword in defiance.

"I am ready too, sire," Wolf announced, and let out a

howl like a war cry.

"AWOOOOOooooooooooooooo!"

"I was born ready!" Bubbles chimed in and everybody turned to look at him with surprise. Nobody was more surprised than Bubbles, who soon realised his mistake.

"Oh. Sorry, I meant to say I was born *Freddie*. That was the name given to me in the pet shop before Rose bought me. I prefer Bubbles FYI. Just in case you were wondering."

Wolf rolled his eyes and Bubbles continued to witter on as the gang set off on their final assault on Fort Doom.

They were steady,
they were ready,
And one of them
was once called Freddie.

CHAPTER TWENTY-EIGHT

STRANGERS, DANGERS
AND
TREASURE CHAMBERS

Meanwhile, inside Fort Doom, Kris and Vanhessa waited silently in the tower for their rescue party to arrive. The walls were too thick to break through and the door was impossible to force open, even with Vanhessa's strength.

Druilla had something else on her mind. She knew that Merdyn, Rose and the gang were almost there but she was more worried about the two shadowy figures that were now making their way through Skeleton Valley.

They must be tracking Merdyn, she concluded. But the image was still clouded. She could just see arms and legs moving but no facial features. She couldn't even tell if they were male or female.

She was irritated that her magic could not let her see their identities, but she decided to postpone thinking about this for now, especially when she heard the howl of a wolf.

She put her crystal ball away as an agitated Vanheldon walked in.

"Did thou hear that?!" he blurted. "That is Merdyn's Wolf if I am a Vandal."

"So what?" snarled Druilla.

Vanheldon stopped himself. He was being more like a little girl than a warlord. "So . . . I'm . . . just saying. He is nearly here."

"What is it, Vanheldon?" asked Druilla. "Do not be ashamed to be afraid. If we are to be partners, we must shareth all."

"Weeeell." Vanheldon let it all out. "It's just . . . last time I faced Merdyn the Wild I lost every one of my soldiers bar my daughter and my two guards. And that's because they were on the toilet when Merdyn attacked. What I'm saying is that maybe we are a little short on manpower – no offence."

Druilla went deep into thought. "Hmm," she said at last. "Do thou have any objects that belonged to thy dead soldiers? Clothing? Trinkets? Something they have touched; it matters not how lightly. I need . . .

their spirit only."

Vanheldon remembered that he had just the thing.

Shortly afterwards his guards plonked Vanheldon's chest down in front of Druilla and opened it. Inside were hundreds of bejewelled bracelets, necklaces and other treasures – the spoils of war!

Druilla drooled as she ran her hands through the treasure. "These are perfect. From them I can build thee a new army."

Vanheldon almost felt emotional for a moment. "Thou meanst thou can bring them back from the dead?"

Druilla's blue eyes lit up with cruel menace. "Sort of," she said enigmatically.

Vanheldon hoped to see
his brothers,
But it would be an army
like no others . . .

CHAPTER TWENTY-NINE

IT'S ALL IN THE EYES ... MERDYN GETS A SURPRISE!

When Merdyn, Rose and the others finally arrived at Fort Doom Rose felt what Kris must have felt as he approached the dreaded place on Vanhessa's back (except Rose wasn't in a sack). She shuddered at the sight of it.

The place was fortified by a ring of wooden stakes with gruesome animal heads on them. The fort itself was made from sharpened stakes that jutted up like a pointy cityscape at sunset.

Looming above the fort was a watchtower with two enormous bullhorns sticking into the sky. Black clouds – the Tarnish – swirled above the fort menacingly.

"How on earth do we get into this place?" Rose wondered out loud.

"Er . . . through the door maybe?" It was Bubbles.

Rose thought this was one of his sarcastic remarks until she saw the huge wooden doors to the fortress were indeed open. "Why have a fortified wall and then leave the doors wide open?"

Arthur shrugged and Merdyn looked worried again.

Bubbles preferred to look on the bright side. "Maybe there's no one in?" he suggested. "Maybe we can just walk in there, get Kris and – abrakaboom! – we go home."

Wolf rolled his eyes at the guinea pig. He had rolled his eyes at Bubbles so many times now he was in danger of getting a detached retina.

"I think they knoweth we are coming," said Merdyn ominously. "But we have no choice. Arthur? Rose? Are ye ready?"

"Leadeth the way," Arthur said, and they all walked

through the open gate into Fort Doom.

They found themselves in a courtyard, empty save for the Tarnish that stained the ground black. It was quiet. Eerily quiet.

"Kris?!" Rose shouted eventually. "Kris, are you here?!!"

"Worry thee not, the boy is unharmed . . ." boomed a voice that definitely did NOT belong to Kris. Vanheldon strode through a doorway into the courtyard, flanked by his two guards.

Merdyn winced at the sight of his great foe but was glad there were only three of them to defeat. Vanheldon and his guards marched towards the gang and stopped about two horse lengths in front of them.

"Greetings, Merdyn, mine old friend," he said with a smile.

"Thou art no friend of mine, Vanheldon," Merdyn replied.

"Indeed! Thou art an enemy of Merdyn the Great!" Arthur trumpeted, ready for a fight. "And an enemy of Merdyn the Great is an enemy of King Arthur of Albion!"

227

And with that Arthur twirled his sword artfully before adding, "Prepareth to die, thou—"

But his bravado was halted very abruptly by the sound of clinking metal.

SHWUNK, CLINK, SHLINK!

Merdyn, Rose, Arthur, Bubbles and Wolf were astonished to find themselves suddenly surrounded by a hundred soldiers wearing armour from head to toe.

Their armour was as black as the Tarnish that swirled around it. It was almost like it was *made* from the Tarnish. You couldn't see a single feature of the actual soldiers. Their faces and hands were completely covered with armoured plates, which only enhanced their scariness.

"—thou . . . person with a scary army . . ." Arthur finished his sentence.

"Now," said Vanheldon, a smarmy look on his face, "I shall ask YOU to prepare to die. Soldiers? Attack!!!"

And with that Vanheldon stepped backwards and leaned against a wooden post as the army moved with alarming speed towards Merdyn, Rose and Arthur.

CLINK, CLANK, SHWINK!

Wolf bit an approaching soldier's arm, slowing him down, but the other soldiers kept coming.

Arthur attacked them with his sword –

SLICE, SWISH, SWOSH

– sending soldier after soldier flying into the wooden walls around them. But instead of staying down they just got back up and started moving robotically forward again!

Merdyn pointed his staff and threw fireball after fireball at the soldiers.

BLAST!
FLASH!

But the army of faceless armoured soldiers just got back up and kept coming.

Rose made herself invisible then reappeared again, but THWACK! She was hit on the arm by a soldier wielding a mace*.

Rose THUMPED against the side of the wooden fort and Bubbles spilled out of her bag. He hid behind a giant catapult as Rose got back up, rubbing a very sore arm, and started firing lightning bolts of her own.

----
*A mace or "bludgeon" is a weapon with a wooden handle and a thick piece of wood or metal on top.

Rose kept blasting the soldiers, but they came back relentlessly. She used the last of her herbs to summon a really huge lightning bolt.

"HOLCUS GIGANTICUS CRACKAJACKA!"

She hurled it at a soldier and his armour flew apart. But to Rose's horror the pieces of armour all started coming back together, just like the stone hands had done in Skeleton Valley.

"There's nothing inside the armour!" Rose shouted.

"The armour is enchanted!" called Merdyn. "'Tis the darkest magic I have ever seen!"

"I'm out of herbs!" Rose cried.

"Useth the light, Rose! Thou must useth the light!"

"Merdyn, I can't!" she screamed back, fending away another soldier with rocks she picked up from the floor.

"Summoneth the light, Rose!" Merdyn yelled again. "Thou can do it! I believe in thee!"

From behind the catapult Bubbles saw Wolf get kicked

across the dusty courtyard floor – YELP!

A soldier stood over the stricken Wolf and raised his mace. Bubbles didn't like Wolf one bit but he didn't want to see him dead! With one almighty bite he cut through the catapult's restraining rope and sent the giant stone flying. It THWACKED into the soldier.

THWACK!

Wolf got to his feet and nodded "thank you" to Bubbles, then he took off after another soldier.

Rose tried as best she could to summon the light while fending off enchanted suits of armour. She closed her eyes. Tried to think about nature. Tried to FEEL nature. But she couldn't do it. A sob escaped her. She just wasn't good enough at magic.

Vanheldon and his guards laughed heartily.

Our heroes fought as hard as they could, but, alas, they were simply outnumbered and soon found themselves surrounded by the devilish soldiers.

Two of the Tarnished foes each held Merdyn, Rose and Arthur. Another soldier held Wolf, a hand clasping his muzzle. Bubbles stayed hidden behind the catapult, feeling that his heroics were maybe done for the day.

Rose knew she'd let the injured Merdyn down. Surely she could have done better?! Merdyn believed in her and she had failed him again.

Vanheldon finally stopped laughing, peeled himself away from his post and came forward with his guards. He walked up to Merdyn and bent down to sneer at him.

"I've waited a long time for this," he said and took his sword from its sheath.

SHWING.

"Thy magic cannot save thee now," he said, and he drew the sword back ready to plunge it into Merdyn.

"No!!! NO!!" Rose yelled, realising that her great friend and ancestor had only moments left to live.

Arthur kicked his legs and tried to free his arms from the enchanted armour that held him, but it gripped all the more tightly. "Thou cannot do this to him! Thou cannot killeth Merdyn the Great!!"

But none of these protests mattered to Vanheldon. He drew the sword back as far as he could above Merdyn when

– SHWUP!!!

Vanheldon's face froze for a moment, then his eyes grew HUGE and bulged out of their sockets. His legs buckled backwards and he turned green. Then he went to speak but . . .

"CRRRRROOOAK!" went his voice, rather like a toad. In fact, thought Rose, he was looking more and more like a toad by the second.

Vanheldon's guards stood with their mouths wide open as Vanheldon's huge body started to shrink, his skin turning slimy, his tongue growing long and hanging out of his mouth. Then suddenly – SHWUP! SHWUP! – the guards turned into toads too.

Arthur and Rose looked at each other and gasped. Out of nowhere they had been saved. But by whom? Who had been their guardian angel? Their fairy godmother? Their knight in (shining not Tarnished) armour?

Merdyn was wondering this too and he watched as someone else joined them in the courtyard. The figure walked calmly towards him.

To Rose and Arthur she looked like a kind lady. The skin around her eyes crinkled as she smiled, her blue eyes sparkling. But to us she looked just like . . . Druilla.

But to Merdyn she looked like someone else entirely as she approached him, bent down and lovingly touched his face.

"Mother?" he said softly.

"Hello, Merdyn," she replied tenderly. "My son."

From behind the catapult Bubbles's mouth fell open and he spoke for everyone when he said . . .

> *With his heart*
> *a-drumming,*
> *"Wow!*
> *I did NOT see that coming."*

CHAPTER THIRTY

MUCH CONFUSION
AND AN
UNLIKELY REUNION

I must tell you that I am as shocked as you are by this twist in the tale. Suddenly Druilla, the evil sorceress we met in chapter three, seems a world away now. She looks younger for a start, thanks to feeding off Kris's magic, and now we can see the resemblance to Merdyn. Those piercing blue eyes, those high cheekbones, the narrow nose. Goodbye, old hag, hello, fairy godmother. Or just "mother" in Merdyn's case.

She took a glass jar from her pocket and placed the three croaking toads (formerly Vanheldon and his guards) inside it and put it back in her pocket. Then she addressed the enchanted soldiers.

"Take our guests to the guest quarters," she said, gesturing to Rose and Arthur. "I wish to speaketh to my son in private."

The soldiers started to march the bewildered trio to the guest quarters, wherever they were. But Merdyn was not happy.

"I wish my friends to stay with me," he said, a trace of suspicion in his voice.

"What's the matter, Merdyn? Do thou not trust thine own mother?" Druilla said, as if ice wouldn't melt in her mouth.

"Thou meanest the mother who abandoned me as a child. Who left our family in order to find enlightenment?" Merdyn looked around him at the blackened sky, at the Tarnish that diseased the ground he was standing on. "It does not look like thou foundest it."

Druilla gave him a rueful smile like she'd been expecting this.

"Yes, my son. I did findeth enlightenment. It may not be as others know it, but wisdom cometh in many forms. There is no need to fear. My goals are the same as thine: that the world can liveth in peace and harmony."

"Sendeth Rose and her brother back to their time, then we will talk."

237

"Patience, my son. The Rivers are arduous. Kris is well fed and watered. Let Rose have food and rest while we speak. Besides, I may needeth her help."

"Help for what?" asked Rose. "I'm not helping the person who kidnapped my brother!"

"The person who kidnapped thy brother is in this jar!" she protested, tapping the jar of toads in her pocket. "Please. I am not the bad person here. I am trying to helpeth thee! And I needeth thy help in return. There are two people coming, not far behind thee. They have been following thee since thou set off. They will be here any moment and I feareth they meaneth us all harm."

She seemed frightened as she said this – but I'm not sure I believe her, do you? – and ordered her soldiers to shut and bolt the gates to the fort before turning once again to Merdyn. "Please, my son, trusteth thy mother, won't thou? I did ask thee to cometh with me, but thou choseth to stay with thy father. That was not easy for me. Can thou not at least give me audience? To explaineth myself to thee at last?"

Merdyn looked at Rose and Arthur. "All will be well,

238

my friends. Go and get some rest. She's right, Rose. Thou needest thy strength for the Rivers of Time."

And so the soldiers took Rose and Arthur away while Merdyn took Wolf to talk with his mother.

Bubbles had watched the whole drama unfold from behind the catapult. He didn't know what to make of it. Druilla seemed OK, but he was suspicious.

I agree with Bubbles. There's something very fishy going on, don't you think?

She is his mother.
I understand his fluster.
But I'm not sure Merdyn's
right to trust her!

CHAPTER THIRTY-ONE

A MOTHER'S PRIDE
AND
MUCH MORE BESIDE ...

Druilla took Merdyn into the main room just off the courtyard and sat him down by a fire. She had an enchanted soldier fetch some hot tea and then looked at her son proudly.

"Merdyn the Great, eh? I'm so proud of thee, my son."

"I wish I could say the same for thee," said Merdyn sadly. "All these years thou never gotteth in touch with me. Even after Father died? Did thou not care about us?"

"Oh, I did," Druilla replied, hurt. "I thought about thee every day. And I kneweth someday that I would see thee again. And I did."

"A peculiar way of seeing me again. Helping Vanheldon kidnap my descendant. Thy descendant too!"

"But don't thou see, Merdyn?" his mother pleaded. "I kneweth Vanheldon would never stop until he had killed thee. So I tricked him. I tricked him into thinking I was helping him, when all along I planned to get rid of him." She pulled the jar of toads out of her pocket and put it on the mantelpiece. "My two great desires were to stop Vanheldon and see my son once again. And I have done it. I calleth that two birds, one stone."

Merdyn let out a laugh. "My favourite . . ."

His mother finished his sentence. "Type of soup?"

Then they both laughed and drank their tea. It had been a long time since Merdyn had laughed with his mother and, oh, how he regretted losing her.

"I have missed thee, Mother," he said softly. He sounded like he was eight years old again.

"Well, thou don't have to misseth me any more," she said, looking at him with dreamy eyes. "Forget the past. We are together again now and that's all that matters. Thou can stay here with me now. Mother and son together. With thy powers and mine, together we can bring harmony to the earth. Together again, Merdyn."

As much as Merdyn was glad to hear warm words from his mother at last, and as much as he had longed to see her again, he had to decline her invitation.

"Mother, I cannot stay here with thee," he said finally. "I have a wife. I have two wonderful children. I have Arthur to guide to greatness. I have Albion. 'Tis my home."

"Nay! A child's home is with his mother!" pleaded Druilla.

"Aye! When he is a child. When he needeth her most. And thou ranneth away."

"I gaveth thee a choice . . ."

"Aye. And thou art doing it again! And 'tis the same answer. My home is in Albion with my family." Merdyn stood up. He had tears in his eyes. "Now I must sendeth my great great great lots of times grandchildren back to their time. If thou can tell me where the boy Kris is, I will be on my way."

Wolf, who had been sitting by the fire eating a bowl of pottage that Druilla had given him, got up and stood by his master's side.

Druilla sighed wearily. "Aye, I thought thou might sayeth that," she said at last. "Thou art a stubborn, ungrateful child like most younglings. I couldn't change thy mind when thou decided to stay with thy father and I knew I wouldn't change thy mind now either . . . which is why I poisonethed thy tea."

Her words hit Merdyn like a thunderbolt. But that was nothing compared to what the poison did to him as soon as it hit his belly. Merdyn convulsed and doubled over. He fell to his knees as the poison twisted his intestines.

He trembled. "What have thou done to me?!"

"Just a little obedience spell," she said casually.

"W-what kind of a mother art thou?" Merdyn stammered. "I HATE thee!"

"All the better!" Druilla cackled, her true evil self emerging at last. "Hate is good! It feedeth the

Tarnish! Maketh it stronger!"

Merdyn writhed in agony, the potion taking hold of his body. He shuddered one last time then fell silent, his eyes closed. When he opened them again Wolf saw that they were not Merdyn's eyes. They were grey black, like lumps of coal. He was hypnotised.

"Now," spoke Druilla gleefully, "shalt thou do what Mother says for a change?"

"Yes, Mother," Merdyn replied flatly.

Wolf was outraged. "Thou wilt never get away with this!!" he barked, before he too felt sick and his doggy body convulsed. He looked at the bowl of pottage he'd been eating and realised *that was poisoned too.* His eyes went black and he stopped snarling.

He felt like a dog who had very much dropped his bone.
"My mistake.
Thou WILT get away with this,"
he spoke in a monotone.

CHAPTER THIRTY-TWO

LOSSES, DOUBLE-CROSSES AND WHO'S THE BOSSES?!

While Merdyn was being hoodwinked by his own mother, Rose and Arthur were taken to the tower, up some rickety stairs and thrown in an empty wooden room by the silent enchanted soldiers.

"Hey!" Arthur yelled. "I thoughteth we were getting food and drink?"

Rose was more worried about Bubbles. She realised he must have slipped out of her backpack. All that was in there was his Dictaphone. She pressed rewind then played the last entry Bubbles had made.

". . . not having a good time here. Who willingly walks into a place called Fort Doom? Who literally does that? Hang on, zip's opening. Whoa!" Click! Then it ended.

Rose turned to the armed soldiers still at the door. "I've lost my guinea pig!" She started to describe him.

"He's yellowy-coloured, about this long and—"

THUNK! The guards slammed the heavy wooden door behind them and bolted it shut.

"What the—?" Now it was Rose's turn to realise something was wrong. "Let us out!! And, hey, where's my brother?!"

But the enchanted soldiers just marched off. CLANG, CLONG, CLANG!

"HEY, YOU!!!!" Rose shrieked as loud as her lungs and mouth would allow. But they did not return. Then, out of the silence came a muffled sound.

"HMMMMUHMMMMHUHMMM! HMMMM!"

Despite the lack of nuance Rose was sure she recognised the sound. "Kris?!" she cried.

"HmmmmmyeeeH!" came the reply.

"Over here!" shouted Arthur and showed Rose a tiny window. The window had bars on it, but through it Rose could clearly see Kris. Rose's heart soared! Kris! He . . . had no mouth, but he was still alive! Her idiot brother who was nothing but infuriating to her was alive and she couldn't have been happier!

She realised he must've had the lip-seal spell put on him, but that was OK because she knew how to reverse that. She searched her herb belt. It was empty but if there was even a speck of dandelion root she could undo the spell. YES!! She found some, threw it between the bars and chanted for all she was worth.

"FICANTUS! SILENCIO! LIPSEALUS! REVENTIM!"

Both Kris and Vanhessa's mouths returned to normal.

"Rose!! Am I glad to see you!"

"Not as pleased as I am to see you!" Rose panted back breathlessly. "I'm sorry we fought. I'm sorry about everything—"

"Sis! You don't have to be sorry about anything! I'm just so glad you're here. I mean . . . I wish we weren't in prison and Druilla hadn't stolen my magic but . . ."

Rose tried to get her head around this news. "Wait . . . Druilla STOLE your magic?"

"Yep," answered Kris. "Druilla's a baddie."

"Listen not to the one called Druilla!" Vanhessa chipped in.

Kris realised he was being rude. "Oh, Rose meet Vanhessa. Vanheldon's daughter."

"Vanheldon's what?!" Rose could not compute this either. Her brain was crashing with all this new information.

"No, it's OK, she's cool. Although she did kidnap me," Kris reassured Rose. "Who's this guy?"

Rose realised she hadn't introduced Arthur either. "This is . . . er, well, there's no other way of saying it. This is King Arthur," she said, barely comprehending the words coming out of her mouth.

"Hi," said Arthur, casual as you like. "Very cool to meet thee, Kris."

"WOW!" was all Kris had to say.

"Please, Rose?" begged Vanhessa. "Can thou tell me, how is my father?"

"I'm sorry," said Arthur, volunteering to tell her the bad news. "Druilla turned him into a toad."

"A toad? No!!" cried poor Vanhessa. "That evil witch betrayed him!!"

"Hang on, so, this whole thing is not Vanheldon's fault?" asked Rose.

"Nay!" said Vanhessa. "I meaneth, yes, my father wished to have revenge on Merdyn but kidnapping thee? It was Druilla's idea."

"Whoa, hang on," said Rose, now totally confused. "So the plan was to kidnap me?"

"Of course, sis," Kris said. "Why would they want to kidnap me?"

"Because you're so much better at magic than me," said Rose.

Kris couldn't believe what he was hearing. "Sis, I know we argued and stuff, but *no one* is as good as you. I learned everything from you. I look up to you. I'm just sorry I never admitted it until now."

Rose felt a rush of emotions run through her body. What a fool she had been. She was good at magic. Kris said so. And now Kris had lost his magic? Not long ago that would have been a dream come true for Rose, but now she wished more than anything that she could get it back for him.

She pulled herself together. She didn't have time for this right now. She needed to work out what to do next.

Right now Druilla was probably tricking Merdyn into helping her – or worse.

"Merdyn's in danger," said Rose. "We need help. Is there anyone on the outside that could help us?"

"No," Kris lamented. "It's just us."

"Wait. What about the mystery men?" said Vanhessa. Kris hadn't a clue what she was talking about. "Thou knowest? The ones Druilla seeth in the crystal ball? Following thy sister. Have they not arrivethed yet?"

"Druilla mentioned them," said Rose, "but she said they're our enemies."

"No, no . . ." Vanhessa said. "She thinketh they are HER enemies. Coming to save thee."

"Then we need to get them a message," Rose concluded. "Tell them to hurry up."

"But how?" Arthur asked. "We're all stuck in here."

"Erm . . . speaking of getting stuck," came Bubbles's voice. Rose and Arthur looked down at a tiny drain hole where the floor met the wall of the tower, where a very dirty-looking yellowy guinea pig was half sticking out. "Can someone pull me out?!"

Rose was ecstatic. What with the joys of finding her brother alive she'd nearly forgotten she'd lost her pet and best friend. And now here they all were, safe and sound . . . in a prison.

But Rose knew just what to do!

As Arthur pulled the plucky rodent out of the drain, Rose told Bubbles her plan. He was to go and see who the mystery men were and get them to hurry the heck up. If he could bring some herbs back too, that would be great. If they were going to defeat Druilla, Rose would need all the help she could get.

"Anything else?!" Bubbles asked sarcastically.

Arthur shrugged, not understanding Bubbles's sense of humour.

"Just go," said Rose, helping him back into the drain hole.

And so Bubbles set off on his mission impossible.

Bubbles didn't like to play the hero.
But if he didn't,
his chances of getting home would be zero.

CHAPTER THIRTY-THREE

LIFE'S UNFAIR FOR ONE UNFORTUNATE PAIR

CLINK-CLANK! No sooner had Bubbles set off than the door of the prison cell was flung open and Rose was dragged out by enchanted soldiers. Arthur tried to come to her assistance but was shoved back in and the door was locked again. The same thing happened in the cell next door as Kris was hauled out and Vanhessa was locked back in.

"I know circumstances aren't perfect," Kris whispered to Rose as they were both marched down the rickety stairs of the tower. "But it's so good to see you."

"Nice to see you too, brother," Rose replied, and she meant it. "If Mum could see us now, we'd get a right telling-off, eh?"

Kris laughed. "Yeah, she won't be best pleased."

BOOT! The lead soldier kicked open a door at the

bottom of the tower and marched the siblings into the middle of the courtyard. There Druilla greeted them.

"Ah, my great great great great great blah-blah grandchildren. How are we?"

"You can forget the friendly act, Grandma," Rose seethed. "We know what you are."

"And what is that, my child?" asked her ancestor.

"An evil witch who uses dark magic to get what she wants!" Rose hollered.

Druilla laughed. "Gadsbudlikins! What do they teacheth thee in thy school? That good always winneth? WRONG! I was good once. A better magician than Merdyn's father and I was overlooked! He became court wizard and not me! Thou thinkest that is fair?"

"No," said Rose firmly, "I think that's unfair and the world needs to change but you do that through showing people the way. You can't just get what you want by stealing people's magic!"

"Thou art wrong, little grandchild. As I'm about to demonstrate." Druilla stretched out her long spindly fingers towards Rose's forehead.

Kris knew what this meant. "Watch out, Rose – she's going to steal your magic!"

But before she realised what was happening to her, the guards had tied Rose to a stake. She struggled mightily but the ropes were tied too tight.

Druilla stretched her fingers more and faint rays of light began to stream from Rose's head. Her magic was leaving her body.

"Stop!!" Kris screamed. "Leave her alone!!! Leave her—"

One of the guards holding Kris put his metal glove over the boy's mouth to shut him up while Druilla carried on sucking the magic out of poor Rose.

"Nooooo! Merdyn! Merdyn, help!!!!" cried Rose.

It did at least stop Druilla, as she buckled over, laughing hysterically.

"Ah yes, my son. My good son will cometh and helpeth thee. Oh, Merdyn?" she called out in a sing-songy voice.

Rose was relieved to see Merdyn step out of the shadows with Wolf by his side. But it wasn't the Merdyn Rose knew. He was different, lifeless, like a zombie

in a horror film.

"Yes, Mother?" he said in a slow monotone.

"The girl needeth assistance. Willst thou help her?" Druilla chirped with glee.

"I only helpeth thee, dear Mother," replied Merdyn faithfully.

This wasn't the real Merdyn. Rose knew Druilla had done something terrible to him. She'd put a spell on him. Hypnotised him.

Rose and Kris struggled against their captors one last time but they couldn't wriggle free.

"Ye can not escape, my children. Now, where was I?" said Druilla, pondering, and raised her hand to Rose's head again.

> *Kris was horrified;*
> *his sister's situation was tragic.*
> *There was nothing he could do*
> *as Druilla stole her magic!*

CHAPTER THIRTY-FOUR

TROUBLE DOUBLES FOR A SQUEAKING BUBBLES

"Must get help, must get help, must get help!" repeated Bubbles as he sped away from Fort Doom. Above his head the clouds turned black as Druilla spread her Tarnish even further. She became more powerful as she took poor Rose's magic and even the grass beneath Bubbles's feet began to blacken and turn to ash.

It had been bad enough escaping through the tight Dark Ages drains*, but now Bubbles had to run without a clue where he was heading. All he knew was that he had to find some mystery men who were – WHUMP!

Bubbles had run headlong into a pair of legs. TWO pairs of legs to be precise. He looked at the first pair; they were female legs and they were covered in material a bit like jeans. In fact, they were jeans. He followed the legs down

---

*Which weren't really drains as we know them. Dark Ages drains were just holes that led outside. Often they built holes into window ledges so you could just stick your bottom out and do your number ones and twos in the street. Bad luck if you were standing under a Dark Ages windowsill!

to find shoes that looked just like trainers. In fact, they were trainers. Basketball pumps if he was not mistaken. He knew the brand exactly because they were just like the ones that Rose's mother used to wear. In fact . . .

"Bubbles?" It was Rose's mother! It was Suzy! What in the name of organic granola was SHE doing here?

"'Tis Rose's pet?" asked the other person.

Bubbles frantically looked the speaker up and down. She wore old-style clothes so she wasn't from the future but he recognised her too. It was thingy! Er . . . what was her name?! Bubbles wracked his little brain. Merdyn's wife! Evanhart! It was Suzy and Evanhart! They weren't mystery men; they were mystery women! Suzy and Evanhart were who Druilla was scared of.

Bubbles started frantically telling them both about the extreme danger that everyone was in and that Merdyn's mother was an evil witch who was planning on stealing everyone's magic and taking over the world with her black clouds. What Bubbles didn't realise was that his pinecone had been pulled off his collar as he squeezed through the last muddy drain out of the fort. So all the while that he was trying to explain, to them he was just squeaking like a, well, like a normal guinea pig.

Suzy guessed, not unreasonably, that he was asking how on earth she'd got here.

"I called Uncle Martin," she explained. "We got the Rivers of Time spell from Jerabo's ancestor and Martin sent me to the year 521*. Thankfully, I found Evanhart and we came here together."

"Yes," Merdyn's wife added, "Suzy explained to me that in the future women maketh their own decisions and do not have to stayeth at home and looketh after the children. So we decided to follow and see if we could help. But . . . what art thou saying, rodent? We cannot hear a word."

Bubbles realised he'd lost his pinecone and had wasted the last two minutes of his life squeaking like a normal guinea pig. Then he had an idea. He's seen a silent movie once where everything was MIMED! Yes, he would *mime*

---

*Remember Uncle Martin is W-blood too because he's related to Merdyn. And Jerabo's ancestor is Julian Smith, a hammy magician turned actor from *The Wizard In My Shed*. He made a copy of the time-travel spell just in case his magic ever came back. And this is how Suzy got back in time. Clever Suzy!

the situation.

I will spare the reader the details but I assume you'll imagine what he did if I tell you what Evanhart and Suzy gathered from it.

"Man with beard . . . who does magic? *Merdyn!*"

"Has a me? Suzy? *Mother!*"

"But Merdyn's mother be dead. *Be not dead! Is alive and is . . . a cackling evil witch.*"

"She make . . . *Rose sad!* She put Rose *in prison* – with hair, hair gel, *Kris!* My Kris!

"And boy with sword. Oh . . . *Arthur!*"

"Witch hurt Merdyn. Make him – have funny eyes? Wobbly eyes? No. Tongue stick out. A frog? No. A *zombie. She's hypnotised him!*"

"Bad witch putteth hand on Rose's head . . . to pulleth her hair? No. Not hair, *magic! She stealeth her magic?!*"

"Make everything go black. She bad."

"Now we must go, followeth me. Tap wrist."

"*Watch! No time to lose!*"

"*Let us go!* Do not be slow! *Picketh me up!* Not thou. Her. Suzy. Ah, yes!"

Suzy picked Bubbles up and they raced towards the fort which they could now see on the horizon.

I think we need a breath,
time to pause,
And Bubbles deserves
a round of applause.

CHAPTER THIRTY-FIVE

IT'S GETTING FRAUGHT IN THE FORT!

The clouds above Fort Doom were now as black as crows' wings, and thunder and lightning popped and crackled and spread as far as the eye could see.

Druilla had almost finished draining the magic from poor Rose who, like Kris before her, felt as if she were emptying out, like a bath on a Sunday night.

Druilla was pleased with the amount of magic she'd stolen. "My, my," she purred, "what a W-blood thou art, my grandchild! Thou maketh me so strong; thou maketh me so youthful!"

Rose opened her weary eyes to see that Druilla had indeed become so much younger. She looked about the same age as her mother now. He hair was lustrous and bouncy and the wrinkles around her eyes had completely gone. The eyes themselves were even more piercing, her lips were full and her teeth were white and straight and shone like pearls as she laughed uproariously.

"Almost there, little one," she said. "And when I am done thy magic will be gone for ever, isn't that right, Merdyn?"

"Yes, Mother." Merdyn spoke like a robot. "The girl is good but she is weak. She cannot access the magic of light as I can. Nor darkness neither."

Even though she knew Merdyn had been hypnotised, Rose was still heartbroken. Only Merdyn knew she couldn't harness the power of light, and to tell his horrible witch of a mother felt like a deep betrayal.

"Hearest that, little one?" sneered Druilla, really in her element now. "Thy beloved Merdyn thinks thou art weak! He thinketh thou art pathetic. Thou art not a worthy heir to our bloodline!" She turned to Kris. "And as for this fopdoodle? He is not worthy of our name either."

Kris raised his slender eyebrows at her. It was all he could do. But he did it with great sarcasm.

Finally, Druilla pulled her hand away and cut the rope that had tied Rose to the stake. Rose's body fell to the floor empty and deflated like a popped balloon.

"And now," she started, before turning to Merdyn, "my son Merdyn will *kill* his beloved Rose. Won't you, Merdyn?"

"Yes, Mother," said Merdyn automatically and walked over to where Rose was lying. Wolf stood next to him, snarling.

"HOLCUS ..." Merdyn intoned without feeling and slowly lowered his staff towards her.

"No!!!!" Kris screamed and wriggled against the two soldiers holding him. "Please!!?"

Rose and Kris knew what would happen next. Merdyn would say "stonerata" and Rose would be turned to stone. Then Merdyn would utter the oblivion spell and that would be that. She would be gone from the past and the future, from everywhere.

"STONERATA!" intoned the hypnotised Merdyn and pointed his staff at poor Rose – but before the spell could be sent from the tip – SHHHWHIP!

Out of nowhere a bullwhip caught the end of Merdyn's staff and jerked it away. Instead of hitting Rose, the spell struck twenty or so of the soldiers, turning *them* to stone.

An astonished Rose and Kris looked around to see Evanhart (bullwhip in hand) standing beside the door to the prison tower. Then through the door emerged the freed Arthur and Vanhessa, followed by Bubbles (his pinecone now restored) and . . . *their mum!*

"MUM?!" Kris and Rose both said in unison.

"I told you, you were too young to go back in time on your own," Suzy said, unable to resist.

Druilla was furious. She turned to her hypnotised son and the remaining enchanted soldiers. "Merdyn, soldiers, killeth them! Killeth them all!!!"

And then the almightiest battle took place. Evanhart traded lightning bolts with Druilla while Arthur freed Kris and Rose.

As he picked Rose up he gave her a wink. "I was born to rescue damsels in distress!" he quipped.

Suzy then gave Kris and Rose each a huge sharp medieval broadsword to fight the soldiers. "This will never happen again so fill your boots!"

"Cool!" Kris and Rose said together and started battling the enchanted soldiers.

Evanhart stood toe to toe with Druilla.

"What have thou done to my Merdyn?!" she demanded to know as they traded bolts of magic.

"He was mine first!" crowed the worst mother-in-law ever. "Merdyn! Attacketh this woman! Seeth her off!"

Merdyn stared blankly and began to fight his beloved Evanhart.

CRACK! went the lightning bolts. FRING!

went the ice spells. But Evanhart was equal to the hypnotised wizard.

Meanwhile, Bubbles and Wolf faced off together. Wolf was growling.

"Now, Wolfie boy –" Bubbles was trying a nice tactic, even though Wolf was hypnotised too – "don't you remember when I saved your life? Hmm?"

SNARL!

It was clear Wolf didn't remember! He gave chase and Bubbles duly ran, the snarling, snapping Wolf hot on his heels.

Guinea pigs are quite good
at diaries and eating,
But a fight with a wolf
may end with a beating.

CHAPTER THIRTY-SIX

THINGS GO BOOM IN FORT DOOM

The battle raged at Fort Doom for the very future of Planet Earth and darkness was winning. The black clouds of Tarnish swirled above the courtyard. Wolf chased a squealing Bubbles around the battlements. Merdyn traded blows with his beloved wife, but with the power of darkness now behind him he was getting the better of her. Evanhart was backed up against the wall of the fort, panting, as she hurled spell after spell to try to block his.

Vanhessa, Arthur, Rose, Kris and their mum were faring better with the enchanted soldiers. Arthur had discovered that if you severed the helmet from the rest of the armour then it was harder for the armour to reconnect. The armour had to blindly try to find its helmet, which was not easy.

"Throw the heads over the wall!" he yelled. When

they did so the soldiers couldn't find them and so our heroes were at last at an advantage.

Suzy had never been in a magic battle before, so was finding the whole thing very strange but she joined in with gusto. She fought until her broadsword broke then picked up a mace from a toppled soldier and started whacking helmets off with it. It wasn't exactly fun, because they were fighting for their lives – but it was pretty close!

Now, you may be wondering where Druilla was all this time. Well, she was preparing to perform her favourite spell. A spell that needed all the powers of darkness for it to succeed. A spell that she knew would give her the world. People would bow down before her when she used this spell, because it harnessed the power of *fear*. When used upon a person it would burrow around in their minds for their deepest fears like a boar roots for truffles. It was called the NIGHTMARE SPELL.

Druilla stood in the middle of the battle and raised her hands to the black clouds above.

"POLCUS NIGHTMARITAS!!!!!"

she yelled and the clouds themselves seemed to fall down from the sky and enshroud the whole fort in Tarnish. One day soon this is what Druilla would do to the whole world, but the people of this little fort would do for now! Druilla was going to enjoy this practice for the main event.

Kris was the first to experience the nightmare spell. Suddenly he wasn't in the fort square; he was in his classroom. For a second he thought being kidnapped had just been a dream, but then he saw that EVERYONE IN THE CLASS WAS LAUGHING AT HIM. He looked at his clothes. They were hideous. He was wearing a purple shell suit from the nineties. Then he saw his reflection in a window. His hair was permed into curls and was long at the back like a mullet on a death metal rocker. His eyebrows were thick and all mushed into one so it looked like he had a giant caterpillar sitting on his eyes. The whole look was Kris's worst nightmare, which was, of course, the point.

"WAAAAAAAAHHHHH!" Kris screamed.

Rose glanced at him as she fought the soldiers in the fort.

"Kris," she cried, "pull yourself together!!" But to Kris he wasn't really IN the fort. He was in his own worst nightmare.

Suzy was hit next by the spell. She suddenly found herself on stage, with only ten people in the crowd, singing a terribly sad song. She'd always worried that since her husband had died she'd not been the same singer. She was destined to sing sad songs that would drive her audience away. Suzy burst out crying.

Rose turned to see her mother bawling her eyes out. "Mum!!! We need you. Come on!!" But, like Kris, she was gone into a world of her own.

Arthur and Vanhessa went next in quick succession.

Arthur had a vision of his coronation. His crown was made of paper and flew away and he couldn't catch it. All his people were upset. For his worst fear was being a bad king.

Vanhessa started crying because she feared she was about to die in battle without ever being loved. All she'd ever known was war and violence but all she'd ever really wanted was to feel the warmth of a human heart. A hug from her father would do. But now she was going to die without ever knowing what it was like to be truly cared for.

And Bubbles wasn't spared either. His worst nightmare was being chased by a hungry dog, which coincidentally wasn't far from what was happening in real life. Except in Bubbles's nightmare all his fur had fallen off. So not only was he being chased around by a snarling, snapping dog, he was also naked!! It made him poo at a rate he'd never known before, about one every 3.4 seconds, which was a world record for any animal, guinea pig or otherwise.

Rose looked around her at the wailing and crying and gnashing of teeth and wondered what on earth to do when – **BOOM!** – she was hit with the nightmare spell. She was standing in her bedroom in front of her late father. He was looking at her with his bright blue eyes, yet not with love but with disappointment. "You've let me down, Rose," he said. "I thought you were going to be special." Rose burst out crying. She'd only ever wanted to make her father proud. She thought she had done it when she helped Merdyn save the world, but now here she was in the past and she was going to let the world fall into darkness.

If Druilla won this fight, there wouldn't even be a future world to save!!

Evanhart was stunned to see everybody falling apart. Her greatest fear was unfolding right in front of her. It was that Merdyn didn't love her any more and that she would never see her children again. The hypnotised wizard took advantage of Evanhart's momentary distraction and hit her with a fireball. The good witch fell to the ground, coughing from the smoke that had singed her red hair.

Druilla cackled as the Tarnish raged around the fort and spread out across the surrounding land. "It be time, Merdyn. Killeth Evanhart and the world is ours. DO IT!"

"Yes, Mother," said Merdyn, and put his staff to his wife's chest.

Evanhart accepted her fate. She grabbed hold of Merdyn's staff and kept it pointing at her chest, ready for whatever spell he would use to kill her. But she wanted him to know something before she died. She looked him in the eye and said three simple words.

"I love thee."

And then, dear reader, something extraordinary

happened. Merdyn's grey-black eyes flashed blue for a second and he hesitated.

Evanhart noticed. "Merdyn?!" she called. "Art thou in there? Did thou hear me?"

Druilla saw it too. "Merdyn. This is thy mother! Killeth her!!"

Merdyn's eyes went black again and he began the stone spell.

"HOLCUS ..."

But Evanhart knew she'd got to him. "Merdyn? Did thou hear me? I said I love thee!"

Just then, a ray of light burst through the black cloud. It struck the ground by Rose, bringing her out of her nightmare. She wondered what had happened, then saw Merdyn standing over Evanhart. Merdyn looked like his old self again and Evanhart was repeating "I love thee" over and over again. Each time she said it a ray of light burst through the clouds.

That's it! Rose thought. *That's the secret to the magic of light! Love!*

She turned to her sobbing mother. "Mum,

I love you!"

SHUM! Another ray of light pierced through the Tarnish and Suzy came out of her trance.

She immediately ran to Rose and hugged her. "I love you too, Rose!" she said, her heart bursting. "I'm sorry I shouted at you. You're a good kid."

Then Rose turned to Kris, who was wailing and touching his hair. "Kris!" she shouted at him, making him turn to her. "I'm sorry I was a bad sister. I love you!"

Kris stopped crying because his nightmare had ended. But then he immediately began again because of what Rose had just said. He ran to her and Suzy and they had a massive family hug.

"I love you too, little sis," cried Kris. "I'm sorry I was a bad brother!"

SHUM! SHUM!

More light poured through the black clouds.

"I love thee, Rose!" Arthur yelled, understanding what was happening.

"I love thee, Kris!" cried Vanhessa in a move nobody saw coming – except maybe you, the clever reader.

"I love you, Vanhessa!" Kris yelled back. And he meant it too. She'd saved his life after all.

"I love you, Wolf!" squealed Bubbles to Wolf, which took Wolf totally by surprise.

And then, as the light came back into Merdyn's eyes, he spoke to Evanhart. "I love thee too, my darling."

Druilla didn't know what was happening. She looked around in shock.

SHUM! SHUM! SHUM! SHUM!

Further shafts of light burst through the dark clouds, which were now more grey than black, the sun almost poking through them.

Then Rose remembered what Merdyn had tried to teach her about using the magic of light that night with the tarpans. She closed her eyes and thought about the earth, about the ground beneath her feet, about the energy connecting nature. The mountains, the trees, the grass, the moon, the stars were all one. All of a sudden, feeling the love of her mum and Kris beside her, she felt the light gather and glow in her heart. She hadn't felt it that night, but she did now. Light filled her body and she turned to the enchanted soldiers.

"HOLCUS STONERATA"

she chanted, waving her hand and turning the soldiers to stone.

"No!" cried Druilla. "It's impossible! How can she do that?"

Kris looked at his sister with the same question in his eyes.

"I'll teach you one day," Rose said with a smile. "Now let's get rid of this Tarnish for good . . .

BARBARIUM, TARNISH, INVISIBLATIS!!"

she cried, making up a new spell on the spot. To her astonishment it worked!! She threw her hands into the sky and light showered from her fingers, filling the air and obliterating the Tarnish atom by atom!

WHOOOSH!!!

*Suddenly the soldiers and the Tarnish
were gone.
All that remained
was a mother and a son.*

CHAPTER THIRTY-SEVEN

TARNISH IS SLAYED AND AN OFFER IS MADE

As the last swirl of Tarnish disappeared, Druilla once again became the frail old lady who had entered it. Her shiny hair shrivelled and dried up, the wrinkles around her eyes returned and her spine bent so much that she had to reach for a stick to prop herself up. She groaned loudly.

Suzy and Kris hugged Rose again and they all sobbed with happiness. The three of them looked a right state. Their clothes were torn and ripped from the battle and their faces were smudged with dirt.

Bubbles ran up to Rose and literally jumped into her arms.

"Well done, Bubbles," gushed Rose.

"I can't remember what I did but thanks," replied the guinea pig. "Which reminds me. Have you got my Dictaphone?"

Rose nodded and laughed and stroked her ridiculous pet.

Merdyn hugged Evanhart and Vanhessa, not having anyone to hug, hugged King Arthur. This took Arthur rather by surprise but he quite enjoyed it.

"My, my, thou art strong," he said appreciatively. "And . . . a good person. Has anyone ever told thee that?"

Vanhessa blushed underneath her mud-covered cheeks.

"I do not understandeth," Druilla kept saying to herself. "Why? Why has this happened?"

Merdyn broke away from Evanhart's embrace and spoke gently to his mother.

"Because love must triumph over hate, Mother. Light must triumph over dark. If it does not, then nature is doomed."

"What do thou knoweth about love?" Druilla hissed. She might have been an old lady again but she was feisty yet.

"I always loved thee, Mother," Merdyn said. "I still do."

Druilla looked at him quickly. After all she had put him through, he still loved her?

"It is not too late, Mother," he pleaded. "Come back with us; come back with us to Albion."

"Thou could meeteth thy grandchildren," Evanhart added.

"I could even appoint thee court wizard," King Arthur joined in. "If thou promiseth to use thy powers for good, that is."

"You showed us all our nightmares," Rose said. "Now they are offering you a dream. You must take it, Druilla."

"Come with us, Mother. Please?" said Merdyn in one final plea.

Druilla looked weary, like she needed a rest from darkness, from mayhem.

"Thank thee, child," she said to her son gently. "But no thanks!"

And with that she thrust her hand to the ground just in front of her – it burst open in a trice and green light shone out. She gave her son one last look – then jumped inside.

Seconds later, the gap closed, and it was like she'd never been there at all.

She was given a chance,
which she chose to eschew.
Where she had gone,
nobody knew.

CHAPTER THIRTY-EIGHT

TOADS RETURNED, MEMORIES BURNED AND LESSONS LEARNED

And so Druilla was gone, and Rose had helped save the world from darkness once again. But there were still one or two jobs to do before they all said their goodbyes.

First Merdyn had to turn Vanheldon and his guards back from being toads into being warrior Vandals. It was something he was loath to do but Vanhessa insisted that her father would have learned his lesson.

"REVENTIM ANIMA TOADAMODE!"

Merdyn chanted, and Vanheldon and his guards became human again.

"Merdyn the Wild?" Vanheldon said to the great wizard. "Let us let bygones be bygones, eh?"

Merdyn agreed and the pair shook hands at last.

Then Vanheldon turned sheepishly to his daughter

and at long last he hugged her. Vanhessa was so happy to feel her father's love she burst into tears. Eventually Vanheldon released his hug (which was just as well as Vanhessa was nearly out of breath).

"Vanhessa? I oweth thee an apology. I thinketh thou were right, my child," he said. "We WERE the baddies. But not any more. From now on this fort will be known as –" if someone had had a drum, there would have been a drum roll, so just imagine it, please – "Fort Death."

Everybody looked at each other.

"Er . . . that's still a little dark, Father," worried Vanhessa.

"All right then," her father huffed. "Fort Disaster."

Vanhessa shook her head.

"Fort Calamity? Fort Mayhem!"

Vanhessa nodded her head. "Yes. That will doeth well, Fort Mayhem it is."

Then there was the little matter of Vanhessa herself to deal with. Merdyn asked Kris how much he'd told her about the modern world because any information that he'd imparted could have a huge impact on the future.

"I hardly told her anything!" he protested, but after some gentle nudging from his mum it turned out he had told her about:

+ Cars/aeroplanes/space travel
+ Electricity
+ Microwave ovens
+ Fashion
+ Television/cinema/console games
+ Robotics
+ $E=mc^2$/splitting the atom
+ Nuclear fusion

"Kris!" groaned Rose.

With her knowledge of these inventions the world could be a very different place when Rose, Kris and their mum got back to their time. After a short deliberation, it was decided that Vanhessa would have to have the memories of her time with Kris erased.

Vanhessa agreed and looked Kris in the eye. "I'm sorry for kidnapping thee. But despite this thou were good and kind to me and that is something I will never forgeteth," she paused for a second. "Well, I will because thou art to wipe my memory. But knoweth that if that hadn't happened, I would never have forgotten thy kindness."

Kris held her hands in his. "And know I will never forget you," he said softly. "And I actually won't because I'm not having my memory erased."

Rose then took her half of the ripped memory-wipe spell from her pocket. (Remember that this was what had caused the friction between her and her brother in the first place – seems like a long time ago, eh?) Kris took his half of the spell from his pocket, and they put them together. Suzy looked at them proudly.

"Can I just add one thing?" said Rose right before they performed the spell together. "We need to say 'permanento' on the end as the spell doesn't actually last that long."

Kris nodded. "Attention to detail. That's why you're so much better than me, Rose."

"Not better," Rose corrected. "Just different. Now, come on, Kid Magic, we've got a memory to wipe."

"PRIMULA VERIS THINKSWIPEYMEMORALIS PERMANENTO!"

they chanted together and in the flash of light that came from Rose's fingertips Vanhessa's memory was wiped. As soon as it was, she looked at the strangely dressed people in front of her and pulled out her sword.

"What art thou doing in Fort Doom!! Death to intruders!!"

"Whoa, child," said Vanheldon, calming her. "These are our guests at Fort *Mayhem*."

Vanhessa was confused. "Fort Mayhem?"

"We are the goodies now," Vanheldon told her, smiling, which was an expression she had never seen on her father before.

She put her sword away, relieved. "I am glad, Father. It was tiring being a bad person."

Vanheldon had one more thing he wanted to do. He picked up the spoils of war from his long-dead soldiers. "It is time I putteth the past to sleep."

And then he threw the chest full of gold, silver and ruby trinkets down the well.

"Goodbye, my soldiers. Sleepeth tight."

And so it was time for Rose, Kris, Suzy and Bubbles to go home.

"I will misseth our little arguments," Wolf said to Bubbles. "Here's a tip for thee, pig. Never runneth away from a dog. They liketh the chase too much."

"Thanks, Wolf. I'll miss you too."

Then Arthur said goodbye to Rose. "Rose, thou gavest me a new focus. From now on I will thinketh only of being a cool king. And part of that is listening to Merdyn here. Thank thee, Rose, from the bottom of my broken heart."

"You're welcome, Arthur. I know you're going to be a great king. And not just because I read about you in books."

Arthur's ears pricked up. "What does it sayeth about me in books?"

Rose backtracked. "Don't you worry about that. Just

keep doing what you're doing."

Next Evanhart said goodbye to Suzy.

"Thank thee for all thy advice, good Susan. I will take heed."

Merdyn flashed Evanhart a worried look.

"What did she tell thee? Do we have to wipeth thy memory too?"

"Oh, it's nothing that will do any harm to the world," Suzy replied for her, giving Evanhart a wink. "Right, Eva?"

Evanhart winked back. "Indeed."

Then Merdyn said his goodbyes to Kris, and, of course, Rose.

"Rose," he said tenderly, "I thought I'd never be again saying goodbye like this."

"Will it be the last time?" Rose asked.

"It must be, my child," the great wizard replied. "We cannot risk meeting again. Luck was at our side this time but it may not be the next. 'Tis painful for our hearts. But 'tis for the best that this be farewell for thee and I." He stroked her cheek one last time. "Go and spread the light in thy world, my great grandchild."

"I will," she replied, the tears now flowing good and proper. "I love you, Grandad."

"I love thee too, my dear sweet grandchild."

And then the two relatives, who had left each other once already in the future, hugged goodbye for the final time in the past.

Rose wiped away her tears on the sleeve of her hoodie and summoned the Rivers of Time with her newfound magic of light.

"BARBARIS, REVENTIUM CLOCKASHOCK."

And the River opened up, took the mother and two children away and closed again.

A few hours later, down in the then sunshine-drenched village, the flower seller was listening to a man recount the already legendary story of the battle between light and dark at Fort Doom (now Fort Mayhem).

"Aye," said the man. "Apparently 'twas the little girl who was the author of the victory. What was her name? Rose, methinks."

"That's it!" cried the flower seller, having a eureka moment.

"What's it?" replied the confused man.

"I've been wondering what to call these new flowers I found." And she pointed to some beautiful bright red-petalled flowers.

"Give them a whiff.
They smell nice in your nose.
And from now on
they will be called a rose."

CHAPTER THIRTY-NINE

WOOD HAS ROTTED AND DIFFERENCES ARE SPOTTED

Rose, Kris and their mum arrived precisely where they had left. The only difference being, of course, that it was 1,500 years in the future. Modern times. When you and I live.

As their eyes adjusted to the sunlight, they saw a dozen or so gobsmacked faces staring at them. They were the faces of a team of archaeologists who were carefully unearthing the remains of a sixth-century Vandal fort.

Rose thought how strange it was that 1,500 years had passed in the blink of an eye and all that was left was the outline of the courtyard.

Kris noticed that the broken sink stone was still there, though; it had hardly changed at all. The archaeologists would probably never know it had been used by an evil witch to conjure giant beasts and skeleton hands.

"Er . . . where did you come from?" asked the totally

bamboozled head archaeologist.

"Just, er . . . visiting," offered Suzy.

"But we don't open until next year," replied the stunned scientist.

"Well, we're just getting ahead of the crowds," Rose quipped as the family marched out of the ruined fort.

Kris had harboured hopes of digging up the treasure that Vanheldon had hidden and becoming the richest boy on earth, but the sight of the archaeologists made him change his mind. Besides, he'd learned a lot on his journey to the past, not least about being a goodie.

"I'd look down the well if you really want a treat," he told the dig team as he walked across what had been the courtyard. "I'd say it was about . . . here . . ." He pointed with his foot at a stone sticking up out of the mud. The lead archaeologist rushed over and dug round the stone to find even more stones. In a circle no less. It was an ancient well.

She pulled her glasses off her face in astonishment and looked up, but the family were gone already.

"Thanks," she said to no one.

Suzy was a very clever mum and made sure that when Uncle Martin had sent her forward in time, she had put all their passports in her jacket pocket just in case by some miracle they all got back safely.

As they travelled back home Rose wondered whether anything had changed. Had they managed to go back in time and come back without affecting anything in the future?

At first everything seemed normal. But then she began to spot subtle differences. For a start, she saw more men with children and babies. There were dads everywhere, changing nappies, carrying snack bags and looking after toddlers.

Then Rose noticed more women in jobs previously traditionally done by men. Taxi drivers, luggage porters. And when they got on the aeroplane the pilot was a woman.

"As your captain I hope you enjoy your flight with us today and wish you a pleasant onward journey," came the voice across the tannoy. Rose had never flown with a female pilot before.

Then came the clincher. Reading an in-flight magazine, she saw that the president of the United States was a WOMAN. Not only that, she was the *seventh* female president of the US! Rose turned to her mum who was busy writing new songs.

"Mum . . ."

"Just a sec . . ." Suzy said. New songs had been pouring out of her since her adventure into the past. Now she was just finishing a tragic one about a sorceress who had tried to take over the world with dark magic but failed. (I wonder where she got that idea from!?)

She turned to Rose, putting her pen down. "Yes, love, sorry."

"What *did* you tell Evanhart when you were walking together?" she asked her.

Suzy shifted uncomfortably in her seat. "I just said a few home truths about men and women. Men should do more childcare; women should have equal rights and pay in the workplace. Nothing too crazy. I just wanted to, you know, speed things up a bit."

Suzy waited for her daughter to explode, saying things like "You can't mess with the space-time continuum etc."

Rose burst out laughing. "Way to go, Mum!" she said. Much to Suzy's relief.

Down in the hold of the plane, where all the pets were being transported, something else had changed. Bubbles had been placed next to a dog that snarled at him, baring its teeth and salivating like crazy. Bubbles didn't react at all, he just stared at it and said . . .

"You don't scare me, pal."

The dog was so confused it just whimpered, turned around three times in the way that dogs do and laid down. This left Bubbles free to finish his diary entry.

"So what have you learned, Bubbles, on your long and difficult journey to the past, I hear you ask. I'll tell you, and it's profound. I learned this. Never, ever, ever, ever forget to pack a snack." Then Bubbles paused, proud he had given some sage advice to his readers/listeners. "The End," he added, and pressed stop on his Dictaphone.

"Right. A well-deserved sleep, I think," said Bubbles and closed his eyes. During the sleep he dreamed he was the ringmaster of a circus.

But rather than horses,
guinea pigs rode dogs instead,
And the dogs had to do everything
Bubbles said.

EPILOGUE

A few weeks after Rose, Kris and their mum returned to Bashingford something very strange happened. As if our story weren't strange enough! But, no, this was even weirder.

To witness this event I must ask you to cast your gaze across the pond. No, not the pond at the end of your garden. I mean the very large pond that is the Atlantic Ocean. To a place called New York City to be precise. To a place called Brooklyn to be even more precise. And, to be even more precise than that, you need to look inside the jobcentre* on Brooklyn Bridge Boulevard.

In this jobcentre a bored worker called Rob was checking his phone for messages when someone sat down at his desk and put a job card down in front of him.

---

*A jobcentre is a place where people who are without jobs go to find jobs (unsurprisingly).

"What be a 'supply teacher'?" the person said.

Rob looked up to see a woman. Or he suspected it was a woman. Her cloak and shawl obscured her face.

"It's, like, a teacher who fills in for other teachers when they're sick, you know?" Rob explained without much enthusiasm. "What's your specialty area?"

"Hmm," mused the shawled lady. "Alchemy, potions, spells, hexes, curses, that sort of thing."

Rob laughed, assuming she was joking. "Science, huh?"

"Er . . . yes," said the woman.

"Then it sounds like you're perfect," said Rob, sliding the card back to the lady. "Just take the card over there and fill out your name and stuff."

The lady reached eagerly for the card. But Rob suddenly pulled it back.

"Wait," he said. "I'm supposed to ask how you are with kids? Whaddya say? You prepared to shape the minds of the future generation?"

"Oh yes," said the lady.

"Then you're good to go," said Rob. "Good luck."

The lady took the card and pulled down her shawl. She had raven-black hair, piercing blue eyes and high cheekbones.

"Thanks," she replied.

"You're welcome," said Rob. But when he looked at the woman's face a shudder ran down his spine. He had never seen a face like it. As she walked away, Rob felt very peculiar. Who was that creepy woman, he thought?

He shivered in his chair.
He scratched his head like a gorilla.
But you know who it was, don't you?
That's right. It was Druilla . . .

IF YOU HAVEN'T READ IT ALREADY,
GO BACK AND FIND OUT WHERE IT ALL BEGAN ...

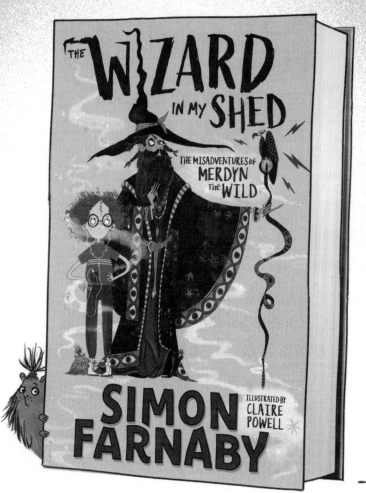

MERDYN THE WILD is from the Dark Ages.
He's the world's greatest warlock (don't call
him a wizard), banished to the 21st century
for bad behaviour, and he's about to create a
whole load of trouble for **ROSE**, aged twelve,
and her guinea pig **BUBBLES**.

CHAPTER ONE

FOUL SMELLS AND MAGIC SPELLS

To begin our story, I need you to cast your fertile imagination back to a time that history forgot. No, not the dinosaurs, that's too far . . . no, not the Vikings, that's not far *enough*, and besides, libraries are full of books on those hooligans. No. I want you to imagine THE DARK AGES. The year 511 to be precise, right in the middle of the Dark Ages, which makes it a contender for the darkest year in all of history.

The Dark Ages were called the Dark Ages not because it was always dark (like Iceland in winter) but because nobody REALLY knows what happened during this time. Nobody wrote anything down or took photos (obviously). The Dark Ages were a time full of menace, mystery and, crucially, magic.

Having said all that, one fact I can tell you is that on

a crisp spring night in 511, King Paul and his justice chiefs gathered at a clearing in a forest near the village of Hupton Grey – a place now known as the Oldwell Shopping Centre, near Bashingford, just off the M3 – for the trial of a notorious criminal. The forest looked a lot different back then, of course. The trees were still there for a start, large and imposing, especially when the makeshift court's lanterns cast flickering shadows upon them.

A crowd of around two hundred people had gathered to watch the spectacle about to happen. The smell would have been intolerable to modern noses, as even noblemen didn't bathe for months on end, and most of the audience were peasants, who rarely bathed once in their lifetimes. They elbowed each other and stood on their tiptoes to see the action. You must remember, there was no TV, and no laptops or iPads in those days. For the local folk, this was the equivalent of going to the cinema. Some even brought snacks. Not popcorn of course, but smoked pig snouts and pickled eggs. A trial of a famous criminal such as this was blockbuster entertainment. And what's more, it was in 3D.

"Will the defendant pray riseth!" boomed the

master of ceremonies.

Gasps rippled through the crowd as the defendant rose all right, but not using his feet! Instead he rose, cross-legged, until he was floating some two metres above the ground. His chains tightened around the huge boulder they were fastened to, making a chilling sound: CRINK! And there the famous felon bobbed, like a human-shaped balloon at a birthday party, eyes closed, a playful smile stretched across his filthy face like a schoolboy who knows he's done wrong but couldn't care less. This is the hero – or should I say the *anti*-hero – of our story. His name? Well, you probably read it on the cover of this book, but just in case you missed it, his name is . . . Merdyn the Wild.

King Paul and his chiefs shook their heads. They had hoped that the presence of Evanhart – the King's daughter – might temper Merdyn's mischievous nature. The two had been friends at the School of Alchemy (Magic School to you and me) until, in adulthood, Merdyn chose the path of darkness. Now Evanhart barely recognised the man floating before her, his robes grubby, his beard long and straggly and his hair matted and adorned with stolen

trinkets. He looked more like a
pirate than a wizard.

"For the prosecution, I calleth
Jeremiah Jerabo," boomed the MC.

The smile quickly fell from
Merdyn's face. Jeremiah Jerabo had also

been at the School of Alchemy, but Merdyn's memories of *him* were very different from his memories of Evanhart.

Evanhart had been Merdyn's best friend and confidant. Jerabo, however, was a jealous snitch. Every time Merdyn had engaged in anything fun, such as turning the teacher's apple into a toad just as he was taking a bite, Jerabo would tell on him. And here he was, at it again, telling teacher! Except this time it was the King, and there was more at stake than a cane on his backside.

Jerabo swaggered to the centre of the court and cleared his throat like an actor preparing for his big moment. He'd waxed his blond bouffant hair into a point and shaved his yellow beard into a goatee, making his head look not unlike an ice-cream cone.

"Merdyn the Wild!" he piped with great pomposity. "Thou standeth accused of multiple crimes against the Alchemist's Code. Thou art a thief, a vandal and a mischief maker who knoweth no bounds. Very few of us are born W-blood . . ."

This is probably not a blood group you're familiar with, but in those days, it was quite common, and basically meant being born a wizard or a witch with magical abilities.

". . . and those of us who art, must use their powers for good, like myself and Evanhart. But thou, *Merdyn the Wild* . . ." Jerabo had reached fever pitch – "I putteth it to THEE that thou have become the worst W of all – a *WARLOCK*!"

And I put it to YOU that you're probably wondering why there are so many thees and thous in that sentence. Well, it was the old way of saying you, yours etc. So thou had better get used to it.

The crowd gasped when it heard the word "warlock". Some felt lightheaded, while one or two even fainted and had to receive medical attention. A warlock is basically a bad wizard, times a thousand. They use their magic for nothing but mayhem.

"That's right," Jerabo hissed. "Do thou have anything

to say for thyself, Merdyn the Warlock?"

This was where Merdyn was supposed to defend himself. This was the moment he could have told them where he had put the giant rock he'd stolen from the ancient Magic Circle (he'd carved the face of Evanhart into it and shrunk it to fit in his pocket). He could have pointed out that the gold he had stolen from the royal war chest had actually prevented the King from starting wars, and wasn't that a good thing? He could have made the case for all his actions, but in truth Merdyn didn't care what anyone thought of him any more. So instead, he slowly lowered himself, put his feet upon the ground and announced in a gruff, powerful voice:

"I AM MERDYN THE WILD!
THE GREATEST WARLOCK OF ALL TIME!
DESTROYER OF ENEMIES!
ALL WHO KNOWETH ME DO BOW DOWN BEFORE ME!

THOU THINKETH THOU CAN CAPTURE ME?"

He let out an almighty howl of laughter.

"THOU MIGHT AS WELL TRY TO SHACKLE THE WIND!"

Never mind gasps, the crowd was now at the part of the movie where they felt genuinely frightened. If there had been a sofa available, they would have hidden behind it. But sofas wouldn't be invented until 1465, so they just closed their eyes instead. It was testament to Merdyn's powers that they felt so scared, even with him chained to a rock the size of Wales.

"Now," said Merdyn in a quieter voice, "if thou will excuseth me, I'll be off." And with that, he opened his tunic to reveal a belt with little leather pouches tied to it. In a flash he took a pinch of herbs from one of the pouches, slapped his hands together – CLAP! – and chanted:

"LYCIUM BARBARUM! GRABACIOUS! THUNDARIAN!"

Thundarian was the name of Merdyn's staff. It had been taken from him upon his arrest, and his plan was to summon it with this spell.

The plan seemed to be working. A great wind swirled around the court and, from behind the chiefs, Thundarian came floating towards Merdyn's outstretched hand. It was a wonderfully gnarled piece of oak around two metres in length, with an intricately carved eagle perched on top.

It was almost in Merdyn's outstretched hand. Had he grasped it at that moment, he would have unleashed all measure of heinous magic on his captors. He would have turned Jerabo to stone, then shattered him into a million pieces with one flick of his finger. He would have turned the King and his chiefs into stinking goats in a thrice. He would have turned on the crowd and magicked their eyes – which were now as big as saucers – into *actual* saucers.

These revenge fantasies were swirling in Merdyn's warped mind as Thundarian got to within millimetres of his straining fingers. But suddenly . . . CRIIINK! Merdyn hadn't realised that there was also a chain attached to his staff. The chain pulled tight, the staff came to a standstill and Merdyn collapsed in a heap, his energy and chance of escape gone.

In the silence that followed came a hearty laugh.

Jerabo had been watching all this with great pleasure.

"I thought thou might try that," he said, and pulled an ornate black and gold spellbook from his tunic. Each witch or wizard had their own way of casting spells and Jerabo, being a stickler for tradition, liked to use a spellbook.

"CASIAN WALLAT FLOATABOAT!"

he muttered, thrusting his hand out, causing Thundarian to drift towards him instead. Then he grabbed Merdyn's precious staff and snapped it over his knee. CRACK.

"Nooooooo!' yelled Merdyn.

Even Evanhart winced at this cruelty. She'd seen Merdyn lovingly whittle that staff over hundreds of hours at the School of Alchemy. Merdyn's heart might have closed off over the years, but Thundarian was the one thing he obviously still cared about.

"Curse thee, Jerabo!" Merdyn wailed. "Thou art a scurrilous coxcomb*!"

Jerabo merely chuckled and threw the broken staff

----

*In case you're wondering, scurrilous meant vulgar in the Dark Ages. Coxcomb referred to a cockerel whose 'comb' is a bright red crest on top of its head. Basically, it's a very long-winded way of calling someone a show-off.

pieces down the stone well that stood in the forest clearing. *Tonk, tonk, tink, tonk, tink, tonk, splosh*, went the broken timber. Then he turned to the King.

"I hope this final act of defiance will convinceth Thy Majesty that we must mete out the very harshest of penalties to this warlock." With great fanfare, Jerabo licked his finger and used it to turn the pages of his spellbook slowly. "The prosecutor recommendeth to the court –"

✳ FLIP – "that he be sent to the Rivers of Purgatory –"

✦FLIP ★ – "for *eternity*!"

The crowd murmured, for they were truly out of gasps by now. Finally, someone was compelled to speak for Merdyn, and that someone was . . . Evanhart.

Everything about Evanhart said 'mellow'. If she were living in the present day, she would no doubt be a yoga teacher, horse whisperer or your favourite auntie. She had long flowing red hair and silver-grey eyes like still pools of calm water.

"Father," she said to the King now. "Please have mercy upon this man. His powers are great. Perchance he could learn to use them for good?"